Semi-Twisted

Isabel Jordan

This is a work of fiction. Names, characters, places and events are the product of the author's twisted imagination. Any resemblance to actual events, places, organizations, or people (living or dead) is coincidental (and would be super-weird).

© 2016 Isabel Jordan. All rights reserved.

DEDICATION

To all who ever doubted and maligned me (and you know who you are). Be patient. You will be destroyed when my Death Star is fully operational.

Praise for *Semi-Charmed*, an Amazon Top 100 Bestseller

"Harper is a heroine you can get behind! She's witty, crazy, kick ass, and amazing! Noah is my new book boyfriend! He's the bad boy we all want and your mom hates but then she falls in love with him too!"

—Indy Book Fairy

"Fresh and fun. Relaxed with a good dose of humor."
—Lanie's Book Thoughts

"Semi-Charmed is well-paced, fun and easy to read."
—TJ Loves to Read

"The hero and heroine were intriguing and engaging."
—Smexy Books

"Holy crap! That was awesome! More please!! Brilliantly funny, sexy, charming, and awesome."
Me, Myself & Books

"If you are a fan of the Sookie Stackhouse books, Buffy the Vampire slayer, and the likes, you will enjoy this book a great deal."
—The Book Disciple

Praise for *Semi-Human*, an Amazon Top 100 Bestseller

"A fun and sexy, sweet and exciting story about a smart, witty and kick-ass heroine, a swoony, intense and equally badass hero."

--TJ Loves to Read

"Harper Hall is…funny, snarky, can handle herself in a fight and never shies away from telling anyone what she's thinking. Long-story-short, this series is worth a read. Just don't read it in public because there are parts that are snort-laugh inducing (and no one looks hot while snort-laughing)."

--Knockin' Books

"The snark, the humor, the sarcasm, the love. This is a well-rounded, well-written novel and an awesome progression for the series."

--Me, Myself & Books

"I went into this book hoping to get the same feelings I got from the last book. I was not disappointed. This book was great from beginning to end. The characters I loved in the last book were there for me again."

--Pixies Can Read Blogspot

ACKNOWLEDGMENTS

As always, thanks to my son who offered tons of great creative plot ideas for this book. (I'll try to write the dog poop cannon into the next book, okay, baby?)

Thanks to my husband for surrendering his home office so I could have a proper Fortress of Solitude. And, oh yeah, the whole "go ahead and follow your dreams, I'll support you" stuff? That was really great, too.

Special thanks to my primary BETA, L.E. Wilson, for talking me off the ledge and not letting me scrap the book all together. Your belief in the characters (and me) allowed me to pull my head out of the oven and carry on. (Which is a good thing, especially because I have an electric oven.)

Thanks to The Design Dude at Knockin' Books for the fan-freakin'-tastic cover art. Sorry for the all the weird photo searches you must've suffered through before you found "the perfect handcuffed dude." He's no Sex Man, but he'll definitely do in a pinch.

Thanks to Renee Wright, editor extraordinaire, for patiently listening to all my self-doubting whininess, all while correcting my egregious spelling and grammar errors. That couldn't have been easy!

Thanks to my parents for having unwavering, unconditional faith in me. I wouldn't be doing what I love today if you hadn't raised me to believe I could do anything.

And last but certainly not least, thanks to all the fabulous readers out there who have followed Harper, Riddick, Mischa, and Hunter on their journey to this point. Because of you, I'm living my dream. "Thank you" seems totally inadequate, but there it is anyway. You guys mean the world to me.

Chapter One

"I'm sick and broken and twisted, Vi. You have to fix me."

Dr. Violet Marchand raised just one perfectly plucked brow and smirked. "I'm a psychologist, Misch. Not Miracle Max."

Mischa Bartone frowned at her friend (and she used the term loosely). "I'm freaking out here, for God's sake. Can't you just *pretend* to be professional?"

Violet snorted. "Professional is boring. I'm more of a let's-cut-through-the-shit kind of gal."

Cutting through the shit must be working for her, Mischa thought, if all the fancy framed degrees and awards on the walls were any indication.

Throwing herself down onto a buttery leather chaise—*this must've cost a fortune*—in front of Violet's mahogany desk, she demanded, "Vi, are you going to help me, or not?"

Violet sighed, taking a seat at her desk. "Of course I am. What exactly is the problem?"

It would probably be easier to explain what *wasn't* wrong with her at this point. But what the hell, she thought, here it goes. "I can't sleep, can't relax, feel edgy all the time." Mischa paused to gnaw on her thumbnail for a moment. "It's like I've misplaced or forgotten something, you know? It's driving me freakin' nuts!"

Violet nodded. "I know exactly what you mean. This morning I was sure——I mean *sure*——that I'd left my flat iron on. But I checked like eight times and it was off. And yet *still*, I kind of feel like I might've left it on." She lifted her palms in the universal what-the-hell gesture. "Weird, right?"

Mischa ground her back teeth together and prayed for serenity that would probably never come. "I'm having a crisis here! Can you focus for a minute?"

Vi cleared her throat and had the decency to look at least a little ashamed. "Sorry. Let's start at the beginning. Why did you come to see me?"

This was a little embarrassing to admit aloud. "My Vampire Council-appointed therapist?" She rubbed the back of her neck. "He kind of fired me."

Vi blinked. "No, really. Why are you here? Why come see me?"

Mischa threw her hands up. "It's the truth! Check the file he sent you."

Violet pulled up the file from her previous doctor on her iPad. She skimmed its contents before her face split into a huge grin.

"I've never actually seen anyone get fired by their therapist," Vi eventually said. "Well, except for in *What About Bob*. Why don't you tell me why *you* think he fired you."

Mischa narrowed her eyes on her. "How would I know? The guy didn't really confide in me. Just said, 'I'm re-assigning your case to Dr. Violet Marchand, effective immediately.'"

She scowled at the memory of the squirrely little turd the Vampire Council had originally set her up with, and the look of barely contained glee on his pinched face when he fired (*oh, excuse me: re-assigned*) her. "The 'never darken my doorstep again' was implied, not stated," she added. "Isn't it all in my file?"

Violet pushed her wire-rimmed glasses up with her index finger before flipping through screens on the iPad again. "Well, apparently you ever so rudely asked him to provide copies of his credentials and references…"

Well, that hardly seemed like a fair criticism. Asking a psychologist where he earned his degree and to confirm how many others he'd help transition into the vampire way of life (or, *undeath*, she supposed) didn't seem like a fire-able offense.

"...and then there was a refusal to participate in the group trust exercises..."

She snorted. She'd be damned if she'd intentionally fall backward, blind-folded, and trust that some quarter-witted stranger in a new-vampire group therapy bitch-fest would catch her. Just because she was already dead didn't mean she wanted a broken neck. And again, that didn't seem like a good reason to kick someone out of therapy.

"...There are also some notes in here about you questioning his IQ..."

Mischa sighed. Yeah, that probably *had* been rude. She'd own that one.

"...and finally, in a total of eight sessions, you refused to talk to him about the night you died and were turned into a vampire, or anything remotely personal."

In her own defense, she thought, the guy hadn't exactly inspired confidence. And he'd seemed more interested in working through the Vampire Council checklist than he was in actually helping her. He didn't really care about her, so why spill her guts to him just so he'd sign-off on her mental stability and let the Vampire Council know she wasn't likely to go on some kind of bloodlust-induced murder spree?

Her mood soured further as she thought about the Council.

The Vampire Council was the undead equivalent of a court-mandated AA program. New vampires, especially ones who'd been turned without their written consent like she had been, were sent through a gauntlet of psychological evaluations designed to determine their mental readiness for the realities of being undead.

If they made it through *that* without staking themselves, new vamps were treated to a series of community college courses that helped them learn the intricacies of being a vampire. The psychological evaluations had been annoying. But the courses? Those really chapped Mischa's ass. She had a 145 IQ, for God's sake, and she'd been forced to sit through 18 credit hours of common-sense advice like stay out of the sun, or risk bursting into flames.

She could've learned that by watching *Van Helsing*. And at least *that* would've given her the opportunity to admire Hugh Jackman's abs while collecting vampire factoids.

The next step in the program was one-on-one counseling with a Council-appointed therapist. And since that pathetic little fuck had tossed her out on her ass, she had to wonder where she now stood. Was she hopeless? Would she always feel like this? More importantly, would she have to start the program over from scratch?

Vi glanced up from the file. "I know what you're thinking, and no, this doesn't mean you have to start over with the mandatory counseling. I'm giving you credit for the hours you've already completed."

If she still needed to breathe, Mischa would've breathed a nice, deep breath at that point out of sheer relief. "Thanks, Vi."

Vi snorted. "Don't thank me yet. I'm a lot tougher than Dr. Frank. And I know you. I won't let you get away with your usual avoidance bullshit."

Mischa crossed her arms over her chest. "I resent that."

"No, you *resemble* that."

Mischa made a mental note to introduce Vi to her best friend and boss, Harper Hall. The two shared the same twelve-year-old sense of humor and love of anything that annoyed Mischa. They'd probably immediately become besties.

"You're a runner," Vi went on.

Mischa rolled her eyes. "I've never so much as jogged a day in my life."

Vi scowled. "That's not what I mean and you know it. When things in your life get tough, you run. You avoid. You…shut down."

Mischa matched Vi scowl for scowl. "I do not."

Vi leaned forward, steepling her fingers beneath her chin. "Okay, pop quiz, hotshot."

"Did you really just quote *Speed*?"

"Answer a few questions for me," Vi continued, almost completely losing her carefully crafted lack of accent in favor of her New York roots. "If I can't convince you the majority of your problems are self-inflicted, caused by your need to run, I'll sign off on your stability to get the Council off your back *and* I'll help you figure out what's wrong with you. For free."

Mischa sat up straighter. She sensed a trap. Violet was—and always had been—one of the smartest people Mischa had ever known. She was hardly ever wrong. And right now? Violet looked about as smug as one would expect a woman who was hardly ever wrong to look.

"All right," Mischa said reluctantly.

"First question," Violet said. "have you contacted your family since your death and rebirth as a vampire?"

Well, that was a stupid question and Violet knew it.

Mischa and Violet had grown up in the same barrio housing project, so they knew each other's tragic backstories.

Violet already knew Mischa's brothers had disowned her when she went to work for Sentry, the covert agency that policed paranormal threats against humans. Mischa was the oldest child, and they never forgave her for leaving home when their mom was struggling so hard just to make ends meet.

And even now, years after vampires came out of the coffin and Sentry folded like a cheap card table, they barely acknowledged her existence. And that was while she was still human. Now that she was a vampire?

She shuddered at the thought. "No," she answered, tone sharper than she'd intended.

Violet glanced up at her over the tops of her glasses. "And did you ever tell your mother and brothers you only went to work for Sentry to make sure they'd be financially stable after your father's death?"

Vi already knew the answer to that question, too, if the smug look on her face was any indication.

Sentry had made it clear when Mischa signed on that no one was to know of their arrangement. She gave them a lifetime of service, and they paid the ginormous gambling debt her father amassed before he stupidly offered himself up as some vampire's dinner in exchange for immortality—a plan that ended in his death. The permanent kind.

So, thanks to Sentry, her family thought their father died in a tragic car accident, her mother was set for life, and her brothers all went to their first-choice colleges on free-ride scholarships. Sure, they thought she was a selfish brat who abandoned her mother in a time of great need, but hey, no need to dredge any of that up now. All's well that ends well.

She met Vi's stare with a defiant one of her own. "No, I didn't."

Vi made a note in the file on her iPad.

Strike one.

"When was the last time you fed?"

Tricky question. She imagined Vi was referring to feeding from an actual donor, and not that she'd admit it aloud, but she just wasn't *ready* to bite a human yet.

Sure, there were plenty of humans these days who were willing to be walking Slurpees for vampires (the crazy bastards found it *sexy* for some insane reason. Mischa blamed *Twilight*), but it just didn't feel…right.

So, she'd joined the ranks of the vampire vegetarians, a small group of environmentally-conscious folks (OK, hippies) who'd pioneered the movement toward bottled, organic blood substitutes. Sadly, such substitutes—while chock-full of nutrients and readily available in every supermarket these days—tasted like a disconcerting mixture of smoked Gouda and, well, what Mischa imagined feet tasted like.

Long-story-short: Mischa only fed when abso-fuckin'-lutely necessary.

Which explained why she could only meet Violet's question with a vacant stare while her brain groped uselessly for the right answer.

"That's what I thought," Violet said dryly, typing another note in her file.

Strike two, Mischa thought.

"How about your powers?" Vi pressed. "Have you made any effort to explore or control them?"

Mischa almost laughed out loud. *Powers*. Picking up the occasional stray thought from a passerby and accidentally shutting down the city's power grid because someone cut her off in traffic and she lost control of her temper hardly qualified her to be one of the *X-Men*.

No, she didn't intend to explore her powers. Ignoring them and hoping they went away seemed like a solid Plan A.

Vi pressed her lips together in a flat line and shut down the iPad.

Strike three.

Well, shit.

"Look, Mischa, those were my easy questions. I haven't even gotten to the hard one yet, and already, I've proven my point. Not letting your family know what's going on with you, not eating properly, and not making any effort to learn to live with your powers are signs that you haven't fully accepted what you are."

She was running from herself, in other words.

Mischa blinked at Vi, momentarily stunned.

Jesus, was this what an epiphany felt like? Like reality had just bitch-slapped you cross-eyed?

And while she was down, confused and shaken, that's when Vi went in for the kill.

"Have you talked to Hunter?" she asked gently.

Mischa closed her eyes against a painful rush of emotion.

Hunter.

Her reaction to any mention of her sire had been consistent since her turning. The waves of emotions always hit in the same order.

Wave one: hunger.

Really, hunger was too gentle a word for the whole body, bone-crushing, gut-shredding pain that tore through her at hearing his name. And she'd come to understand that no amount of synthetic blood would even take the edge off that hunger, because it wasn't his blood she wanted.

It was just…him.

She hungered for him with every fiber of her unnatural being. Felt cut in half without him.

The Council said that was normal. That there was nothing stronger in a vampire's world than the sire/childe bond, and if that relationship was severed, both parties would suffer.

And Mischa was suffering, all right.

That's when wave two (memories) usually hit.

Mischa remembered the feel of strong arms holding her, protecting her. She remembered warm, laughing eyes. She remembered feeling safe and loved and desired for the first time in her life.

She remembered the look of complete devastation on his face when she lashed out at him after he turned her.

That's when wave three hit. And wave three was the worst wave of all.

Regret.

If she could go back to that day, the day she'd died and he brought her back as a vampire, she'd do everything different. She'd been so messed up and confused that she'd pushed him away. Let him think she hated him, when really, nothing could be further from the truth.

"Hunter's being released tomorrow night, right?"

It had been 5 months, 3 weeks, 2 days and—she glanced at her watch—4 hours since he'd been sentenced to one year in prison for turning her against her will.

Not that she was counting.

He had been eligible for early release for good behavior, but apparently his behavior hadn't been, well, *good* since his incarceration.

He was now being released early thanks to a deal she'd made on his behalf with the Vampire Council. It was the least she could do, really, after he'd sacrificed so much to save her.

Vi cleared her throat expectantly, and Mischa blinked back tears and locked her jaw. She'd be damned if she'd cry and spill her guts in a therapy session with the girl who used to eat chalk in kindergarten, even if Vi was the bringer of epiphanies.

Vi sighed and moved to sit next to Mischa on the chaise. Grabbing her hand, she forced Mischa to make eye contact with her. "That *thing* you've forgotten? That *thing* you're missing?"

Mischa sniffled. "Yeah?"

"Did you ever consider that it's you? That maybe you've—for lack of a better word—misplaced who you are?"

She frowned. "How the hell can someone forget who she is? What kind of thing would cause that to happen?"

Vi smiled a crooked little half smile. "Well, dying, for one thing."

Well that sounded…entirely plausible. Positively steeped in what-the-fuckery, but entirely plausible. "How do I…find *me*?" she asked hesitantly, half expecting Vi to laugh at her or crack a joke.

But Vi didn't laugh. "You're going to start breaking all your old patterns. And the way to do that is to acknowledge that your instincts are all wrong."

Mischa opened her mouth to object, but Vi held up a hand, silencing her. "Don't make me prove it to you."

She shut her mouth. Given that Vi had been able to do in ten minutes what Dr. Frank had failed to do in eight sessions, Mischa supposed she wasn't really in any position to doubt her new doctor any time soon. "Fine, I acknowledge that my instincts are all wrong," she said through clenched teeth. "Now what?"

Vi smiled sweetly, which should've been Mischa's clue to be afraid. Very, very afraid.

"Whatever your instincts tell you to do from this point on, you're going to do the opposite."

Mischa blinked. "Did you just propose a therapy plan based on a *Seinfeld* episode?"

Vi nodded, dead serious. "Yep. By going against your instincts, ignoring the need to run, you'll earn different reactions from those around you. I'm betting on those reactions being favorable. Eventually, that positive reinforcement will reshape your instincts into something more normal. Less…twisted."

Again, that was all kinds of fucked up. And entirely plausible.

"You really are a good doctor, aren't you?" Mischa asked, somewhat awed.

Vi smirked. "You're not the only genius in the room, babe."

Chapter Two

Hunter was no prison novice.

He'd done a brief stint in Andersonville Prison back in 1864-ish. He'd been captured, along with about twenty of his fellow soldiers, while fighting for the Union in the Civil War. It took him a week to get himself and his team out of there without exposing the existence of vampires to everyone involved.

In World War I, while fighting for the English, he was captured and held as a POW for a few days in Langensalza before he was able to mind-fuck a guard into letting him go.

And while it couldn't exactly be considered a prison term, he'd spent some quality time (an hour or so) in a Birmingham jail in 1963 after being arrested during a civil rights sit-in.

Midvale Prison, his current residence, actually made him remember all of his other prisons fondly. Even Andersonville was better than this shithole, and it didn't have plumbing.

And unlike the other prisons he'd been in, Midvale was unescapable. The downside of vampires being out of the coffin, Hunter supposed, was that prisons were now actually equipped to handle them. Silver bars that muted their powers, no windows, guards with wooden bullets and stakes…yep. Humans knew what they were up against now, and had adapted to detaining supernatural criminals surprisingly well.

Built in the 1800's in the middle of a lightly wooded area in upstate New York, Midvale looked like it had been plucked right out of a horror movie. The limestone façade was architecturally interesting, but held moisture like a bitch and made the cells cold and dank. The cloudy gray paint on the walls was broken up only by the occasional brownish water leak stain and patches of black mold. The air reeked of mildew, delousing spray, and unwashed bodies.

Cockroaches deserved better living conditions. The place should have been condemned years ago, and if it housed humans, it would've been. But Midvale didn't house humans.

It was a vampire facility.

As soon as he hit the door, he'd been issued a uniform: a dark blue pair of pants and a matching shirt with an orange number on the back. That number was his new identity. Names were irrelevant in prison.

Here, Hunter was 846324.

He laced his hand behind his head as he lay on his metal bunk and closed his eyes, listening to the cacophony of sounds around him.

The biggest complaint among new prisoners was always the noise. Layers and layers of hollow sounds reverberated down the corridors, creating a deafening roar. Guards yelling, prisoners screaming and crying and taunting each other, the constant rumble of the plumbing…it had been known to drive more than a few prisoners to madness.

But not Hunter. He actually enjoyed the noise. Welcomed it.

Most days, it kept him from being able to hear his own thoughts.

His thoughts were the enemy at this point. They taunted him. Taunted him with memories of her voice, warm and low and husky as she whispered his name. Taunted him with memories of her skin, flushed pink from the friction between their bodies.

Taunted him with memories of her telling him she loved him…then memories of her carelessly casting him aside as carelessly as she crushed his fool heart.

He repressed a disgusted sigh. *That* was a perfect example of why he hated his thoughts. They made him sound like a pathetic, depressed fuck.

Logically, he knew he had no right to blame her for changing her mind about being with him. After all, he vaguely remembered being human. The idea of changing into something, well, *not human* and living, forever, with someone—anyone—was overwhelming at best, terrifying at worst. It was understandable. His brain completely accepted her actions.

But his heart? Yeah, he wasn't sure his heart would ever catch up with his brain.

I wouldn't have chosen this, she'd said when she woke up in that hospital and realized he'd turned her into a vampire. *Maybe I wanted to grow old. Maybe I wanted to have babies and grandbabies and a real family. Now I'll never have that. You took my choice away.*

If he lived to be a thousand—which, let's face it, he probably would—he was sure he'd never forget those words. And she was right. He had taken her choice away. He'd been a damn fool to think she ever would've chosen him over a real family.

The smell of garlic and stale sweat announced the arrival of Hunter's least favorite Midvale guard. He had no idea what the worthless bastard's real name was, but Hunter had taken to thinking of him as Napoleon, on account of his diminutive stature, control issues, and irrationally high self-esteem.

"846324," Napoleon said with a smirk, dragging his nightstick along the silver bars of Hunter's cell. "It's your lucky day."

Hunter glanced at him. "Can't see how that's possible with you here."

Napoleon's eyes immediately went cold, but he managed to keep his cocky smirk in place. "How's the thirst today, Kemosabe?"

Feels like I've been gargling fiery coals, thanks for asking.

He avoided the question, opting instead to say, "In that particular taunt, I would be *Tonto*. *You* would be Kemosabe. See, it works as a racial insult because *Tonto* was Native American like me. Try to do better, OK? Be the best racist you can be. Low IQ isn't really an excuse for being uninformed."

The smirk fell and Hunter barely resisted a triumphant smirk of his own.

Napoleon was a blight on Hunter's cell block, a human stain. A quick jaunt through the little rodent's thoughts when they first met told him the only thing Napoleon craved more than wealth and power was immortality. And thanks to Hunter, no Midvale vampire would agree to ever change Napoleon.

One of the perks of being the oldest vampire in the prison? The other vampires respected him enough to do whatever he said.

Napoleon had retaliated by withholding Hunter's blood rations for the past five months.

Fortunately, Hunter was no novice at starvation, either.

He could still remember Napoleon's red-faced agitation when he learned that vampires as old as Hunter only needed to feed a little every couple of months.

When starvation hadn't worked, Napoleon made false reports about Hunter's behavior that extended his stay in Midvale.

Not that he really cared at this point. It wasn't like he had anything waiting for him on the outside.

Napoleon hitched up his pants and spat a wad of phlegm into Hunter's cell. "Your whore managed to get you an early release, maggot. Looks like you won't be running the cell block anymore."

Making sure no one turned Napoleon or participated in gang rapes in the showers hardly constituted "running the cell block,"— but that wasn't really the part of the conversation that Hunter found confusing. "What whore? Who are you talking about?"

"I'm assuming it was the mouthy bitch who brought down a PR shit storm on the whole supernatural prison system and regs around vamps who turned loved ones in a crisis situation."

That made Hunter smile. He only knew one woman who would take on the supernatural prison system and rain shit down on anyone who dared oppose her.

Harper Hall.

Harper had been his friend for years. He could easily see her going to bat for him and securing his early release. "When?" he asked.

"Tomorrow," Napoleon said, unadulterated evil glee lighting his eyes. "If you can survive the night, that is."

Growls and snarls echoed through the corridor and Napoleon's smile grew as he opened the cell door. Hunter immediately scented no fewer than eight vampires. From the sound of them, they were crazed. They'd probably been starved too. They'd be uncontrollable, even with his superior age and power. They would be no better than feral animals.

Looked like Napoleon decided that if he couldn't convince the vampires in his cell block to take him on, maybe the ferals from the lower levels would give him a shot.

Hunter sighed and slowly stood up, rolling his head from one side to the other.

It was going to be a long night.

Chapter Three

Mischa walked into the lobby at Harper Hall Investigations clutching her iPhone in one hand, and a bag of greasy, reeking chicken wings in the other. She dropped the bag on the reception desk and wiped her fingers on her jeans.

Leon Steinfeld, Harper's office manager, didn't look up from his computer screen as he said, "Don't leave that there. Last time someone left food for her on my desk, she accused me of stealing her fries."

Mischa flopped down on the ratty orange leather loveseat Harper refused to get rid of. "You used to embezzle for a living, Leon. It's not such a stretch to think you'd steal her fries."

He glanced at her over the tops of his glasses. "I'd never embezzle from Harper, and I'd never steal her fries. Especially after she threatened my life."

Misha scoffed. "You're being dramatic."

His brows—well, *brow*, she supposed. Leon really only had one that covered both eyes—flat-lined. "She pulled her sword on me," he said dryly. "If Riddick hadn't shown up with the fries, I might've ended up on the wrong side of a *Highlander* moment."

Harper was eight months pregnant and had an appetite that would awe a lumberjack. The sheer amount of food she could put away defied science.

So these days, Mischa spent about as many working hours going on snack runs for Harper as she did skip-tracing bail-jumping vampires and shifters. And when Harper didn't get exactly what she was craving? Yeah, things got a little dicey. She couldn't be sure that her hyper-hormonal boss wouldn't kill a guy in some kind of fry-induced haze.

She pulled the bag off Leon's desk and dumped it next to her on the couch, just to be safe. Jerking her chin toward Harper's closed door, she asked, "She's not in there with Riddick again, is she?"

Another thing Harper's hormones seemed to crave these days? Her husband and business partner, Noah Riddick. Mischa had read that pregnant women often had an increased sex drive, but the sheer number of times she'd caught Harper and Riddick mid-quickie on Harper's desk was mind-boggling.

Leon pushed his glasses up his index finger. "No, thank God. I paid extra for the cleaning people to Clorox the hell out of that office every night, but I still wouldn't advise ever letting anyone with a black light in there."

True enough. There probably wasn't enough Clorox in the state to rid that desk of all the bio stains it must contain. She shuddered. "So, who's she in there with?"

"Prospective client. Some Pepto-Bismol-wearing, plastic-looking chick. Reminded me of the Malibu Barbie my sister had growing up."

The outer office door banged open, and Benny Scarpelli strutted in and winked at Mischa. He shifted Harper's food to the other side of the couch and flopped down next to her. "Hey, hotness. How you doin'?"

Benny worked for Harper on a freelance basis, handling overflow investigative work when everyone else was busy. He was a halfer, a rather unfortunate vampire/wererat hybrid with a penchant for tasteless jokes and sexual harassment. He was also blessed with a personality only Harper could love.

Mischa would normally remove the arm he'd draped across her shoulders and remind him she didn't like being called *hotness*. Usually reminders came in the form of boxed ears.

But after the talk she'd had with Vi, she decided to go with the opposite of her first instinct. She smiled warmly at him.

He cringed and shifted away from her slightly. "Are you in pain or something, doll? What's wrong with your face?"

Note to self: work on your warm *smile.*

Mischa was saved from having to make an awkward reply when Harper's door opened and the…pinkest woman she'd ever seen stepped out.

Vintage pink Chanel suit, pink pearls, pink Prada pumps, pink heart-shaped handbag, pink headband…yikes. It looked like Valentine's Day had puked all over her.

Leon's description had been pretty dead-on, too. The woman had the tiny-waisted, giant-boobed, long-legged, plastic-perfect look of a six-foot-tall living Barbie.

Her golden hair was coifed to within an inch of its life, and Mischa imagined that if she picked the woman up and shook her like a bulldog worrying a bone, that hair wouldn't so much as budge.

Icy blue eyes fell on Mischa and scanned her from the roots of her hair to the tips of her battered Keds. And when they lifted back to her eyes? Mischa felt as if she'd just been judged and promptly found lacking.

Our Lady of Perpetual Pinkness turned back to Harper, who'd just stepped out of the office behind her, and asked in a squeaky Betty Boop voice, "Is this your operative?"

Benny and Leon snickered, either at her voice or use of the word *operative,* Mischa couldn't be sure.

Harper silenced them with a sharp look and told her client, "This is one of my investigators. I haven't determined yet who'll be assigned to your case." Harper patted Barbie's shoulder reassuringly. "But that's not for you to worry about, okay? I promise you, we'll do our best to resolve your situation quickly, Ms. Eisler."

"Oh, please, call me Barbie."

"No fucking way," Benny blurted, then slapped a hand over his mouth, eyes darting from Harper to her new client, panicked.

Leon bit down on his lip so hard he drew blood (Mischa could smell it), and Mischa had to swallow three times to tamp down the laugh that threatened to bubble up out of her throat.

Barbie eyed each one of them with a disdainful glare before turning back to Harper and smiling warmly. "I have every confidence in *you*, Ms. Hall."

Her tone clearly said she had a little less than zero confidence in the rest of them. Which Mischa could understand, since they were all snickering like a bunch of ten-year-olds who'd just heard a fart joke.

When Harper came back in after escorting Barbie to the elevator, she swatted Benny on the back of the head with an open palm. "Christ, Benny, could you have been any *less* mature?"

"Aw, come on, Harper," he whined, rubbing the back of his head. "You know you were thinking the same thing."

She rolled her eyes and motioned for him to move. He jumped off the couch like it was on fire and Harper dropped into the spot he'd vacated with a huge, world-weary sigh.

"Yeah, all right, I get it," she grumbled. "I practically bit a fucking hole in the side of my mouth to keep from saying the same thing when she introduced herself. How can someone look like that and keep a straight face when she tells people her name is *Barbie*?"

Mischa handed her the bag of food, which she immediately tore into like a starving raccoon rooting through a garbage can. "I'm sure all the Botox helps her keep a straight face."

"No Botox," Harper said around an obscenely huge mouthful of chicken. "She's a vampire."

Wow, Mischa's vampire senses really must suck. She'd had no idea. "What's the job?"

"Ever hear of that vampire beauty pageant the Vampire Council sponsors every year?"

Mischa hadn't, but Leon piped up with, "The Miss Eternity Pageant? Isn't that coming up next week?"

Harper nodded. "It's supposed to. Barbie is the coordinator, and she's had two contestants drop out of the competition this week.

Miss New York and Miss New Jersey backed out without giving Barbie a reason. Now they can't be reached. No one, not even family and friends, seem to know where they are."

Mischa frowned. "Maybe they just decided they didn't want to prance around in their underwear in front of men judging them on their poise and bra size."

Leon snorted. "You tell 'em, Norma Rae."

"Norma Rae fought for a labor union, not women's rights, dumbass," Mischa said.

"Whatevs," he muttered. "Hashtag bitter lesbian."

Mischa stood up, a vague idea of tossing Leon out the window taking shape in her mind, but Harper tugged her back down and pointed at Leon with a chicken wing. "No lesbian jokes. If I ever hire a lesbian, I can't have you getting me sued for creating a hostile work environment. And no verbal hashtagging."

"Why not?" he asked. "How could anyone sue you for that?"

"They can't. It just makes you sound like a douchebag and I don't like it."

He mulled that over for a moment before nodding and saying, "Fair enough."

"So if Barbie's concerned, did she call the cops about her missing contestants?" Mischa asked.

Harper finished off her lunch and propped her feet up on the coffee table in front of the loveseat. "They didn't want to get involved. Said the women had every right to back out of the competition and that they didn't really owe anyone an explanation."

Mischa tended to agree, but obviously Barbie didn't. "And what is Barbie paying you to do?"

"She's convinced someone pressured the girls to drop out, but the other contestants aren't talking. She wants me to put someone in the competition undercover as either Miss New York or Miss New Jersey."

"Because maybe the girls will talk to one of their own," Benny added.

Harper nodded. "I'm taking this very seriously. Barbie is convinced someone is out to hurt her girls and sabotage the pageant, which is supposedly a huge money-maker for the state of New York. In fact, I don't just want to send one girl in. I'm thinking I can add a stage hand of some kind, and at least one other attendant or helper."

Mischa's eyes widened. "Wow, Barbie must have an impressive budget."

Harper tented her fingers like Mr. Burns and smiled a Grinch-y smile. "You have no idea. The Council decided to fund her. They're not happy about the police blowing the whole thing off. If it turns out that something happened to those women, The Council lawyers will most likely slice and dice the Whispering Hope Police Department, specifically the Vampire Crimes Unit, in court."

"So who are you sending in, doll?" Benny asked.

Not missing a beat, Harper said, "Well, Mischa, obviously."

Dead silence greeted her pronouncement, followed by riotous laughter. Leon actually slumped over in his chair, gripping his side while snort-laughing, and Benny almost toppled off the corner of Leon's desk where he'd chosen to perch when Harper evicted him from the loveseat.

Mischa failed to see the humor at all.

The laughing eventually died down to scattering of guffaws, and Harper grinned at her. "Just kidding, hon. I knew you wouldn't go for that. Benny, do you think Angela would do it?"

Angela was a young vampire who, for reasons completely foreign to Mischa, seemed to really like Benny. They'd been dating for about three months.

Benny rubbed the back of his neck. "I dunno, Harper. Angela's kinda pissed at me right now."

Harper scowled at him. "What did you do, Benny? I like Angela."

He had the grace to look a little embarrassed as he said, "Let's just say some girls don't like it when you ask them to do certain stuff in bed."

Mischa closed her eyes. *Please don't elaborate. Please don't elaborate.*

"You know," Benny elaborated, "butt stuff."

Oh, God.

"Some girls have a strict exit-only policy, Benny," Harper said, completely straight-faced.

"Yeah. I realize that now."

Harper rocked to the edge of the loveseat and held out her hands in a queenly gesture everyone had come to recognize as her get-me-the-hell-out-of-this-couch gesture. Benny dutifully jumped up and grabbed one hand, Leon the other, and together they hoisted their pregnant boss off the sofa.

When she was on her feet, Harper blew out an exasperated breath that sent her gold-tipped brown curls flying. One hand automatically moved to cup her belly lovingly.

For the first time that day, Mischa took in Harper's appearance. She was wearing her standard maternity uniform: a black knee-length skirt that appeared to be made out of yoga-pant material and a black T-shirt (probably one of her husband's) that stretched across her belly in a way that defied physics. (Fabric just wasn't meant to stretch at the seams like that without busting.)

Harper glanced down, attempting to peer around her belly. "I'm wearing shoes, aren't I? I can't tell anymore."

If leopard-print flip-flops with wafer-thin soles could be considered shoes, then, yes, Harper was wearing shoes.

Mischa knew better than to tell Harper how cute she looked. The last time she'd said something to that effect, Harper punched her in the arm. Hard. Then, she burst into tears in a fit of pregnancy hormones, which meant that Mischa wasn't able to hit her back.

"You're looking good, boss," she said.

Harper scowled. "I'm looking like I swallowed a fucking beach ball."

This, too, was a hormonal trap, Mischa realized. If she agreed that

Harper was indeed huge, she'd get punched. Then Harper would cry. If Mischa told her she was gorgeous and glowing, she'd be accused of lying, then she'd get punched. And Harper would cry.

Mischa kept her mouth shut as Leon and Benny did the only smart thing and ran for their lives, mumbling excuses about places they had to be.

She was fortunately spared from making any comments as Riddick walked in and dropped a ticket from the police station on Leon's desk.

"You got the guy?" Mischa asked.

Riddick grunted. "It wasn't exactly challenging. He was passed out in his car outside the Rag Tag."

He made it sound like dragging a three-hundred-pound werewolf to the police station for violating his parole was no big deal.

But then again, for Riddick, a *dhampyre* (half-human, half-vampire with all the strengths of both races and none of the weaknesses), it probably wasn't.

Riddick stalked over to Harper and proceeded to kiss her silly. When he stepped back, she licked her lips and gave him a breathless "Hi."

He grinned down at her, and even though the smile wasn't aimed at Mischa, it still weakened her knees. Made her miss what she'd had with Hunter. What she'd carelessly tossed…

Nope. Don't go there.

Riddick rested his hand on Harper's belly and smiled down at her, amused, as she animatedly recounted the visit from Barbie.

And when Harper Hall did "animated," she didn't half-ass it.

A minute later, Mischa was practically doubled over laughing at Harper's dead-on impression of Barbie's voice and overblown, sashaying walk, which looked even more hilarious on a pregnant lady.

After the hilarity died down, Riddick asked, "So, seriously, who are you going to send in undercover?"

Mischa wasn't sure whether to be glad that no one seemed to

think she could do the job, or offended. It wasn't like she was a troll or anything. There were downsides to being a vampire, but she'd actually never looked better.

Dying had done wonders for her complexion.

Harper shrugged. "I'll figure something out." She patted Mischa's shoulder. "Don't worry. I was just kidding earlier. I wouldn't make you do it. I know you hate all that beauty pageant shit."

She did. Every instinct she had told her to keep her mouth shut. To let everything keep thinking she wouldn't, or couldn't, do the job.

But in her mind's eye, she saw Violet, smirking at her, looking all smart and professional and…smirk-y.

Mischa squared her shoulders, took a deep breath she didn't need, and blurted, "I'll do it. I'll enter the pageant and find out what happened to the missing contestants."

Riddick and Harper were silent, expressionless, for a full thirty seconds before finally, Harper asked, "Who are you, and what have you done with the real Mischa Bartone?"

Mischa snorted. "I'm not at all sure. But if I find her, I'll let you know."

Chapter Four

As Hunter had expected, a woman was waiting to pick him up when he walked out of the prison.

Just not *the* woman.

She waited for him just outside the guard station, as a guard signed out the meager possessions he'd entered the prison with. Sixty dollars, the green apple Chapstick Mischa had asked him to pocket for her before their lives fell to shit, a poker chip from the casino where he'd last touched her, seen her smile, listened to her laugh...

He scrubbed a hand over his face. Jesus. He really was a pathetic, depressed fuck.

The door swung open and fresh night air hit his face for the first time in months.

Time to start over.

A faint moan drew his attention to the gate. Napoleon stood, hunched over at the waist, hands clutching his groin, face an odd shade of purple.

Harper Hall leaned casually against the building, watching his approach, arms crossed over her hugely pregnant belly. He raised a brow at her and glanced back at Napoleon.

She shrugged. "He got a little hands-y when he frisked me, so I got a little knees-y with his balls."

He grinned and shook his head, giving her a mock salute. "My hero."

He gestured for her to go ahead of him, and they exited the prison together.

Napoleon gurgled something unintelligible and shut the gate

behind them. Hunter didn't really care what the fucker might be trying to say, but he imagined it was directed at Harper, and he couldn't let that stand.

He stopped and glanced backward. "Oh, by the way. You never bothered to ask what powers I might have. The powers that were muted by the silver bars in my cell?"

Napoleon's eyes were full of blood as they lifted to Hunter's.

"I can override free will," he said, putting every bit of power and malice and threat he had behind the words. "And I don't need to be anywhere near you to do it."

Some of the defiance bled out of Napoleon's expression, but he wisely, for once, kept his mouth shut. Surely even a complete dumbass like Napoleon realized that if Hunter told him to cut out his own heart, he'd be powerless to resist the compulsion.

"Stay away from me and mine," he added.

There was really no need to say anything else.

But Harper Hall never really let that stop her. "Suck it, fucknut," she tossed over her shoulder.

On the way to her car, she jerked her chin toward what felt like a huge gash on his cheek. "Get in a fight over whose turn it was to pick up the soap?"

Leave it to Harper to make prison rape jokes with a newly released convict. Nice. He gestured toward her belly. "Been letting your looks go since you got married?"

Her lips curled up and she nodded appreciatively. "Nice."

Before he could reply, she threw herself at him and squeezed him with every ounce of strength in her five-foot-six frame. If he'd been human, at least three of his ribs would've cracked.

He stood motionless in her embrace for a moment, arms hanging loosely at his sides. He hadn't been touched in almost a year, and he'd kind of gotten used to it. Having someone so close after so long was a little...surreal.

After a moment of internal debate during which he had to actually remind himself how to behave normally, he wrapped his arms around her round body and returned her hug.

She pulled back and punched him in the stomach, putting her full weight—which was more considerable than it had ever been—behind it.

He grunted and rubbed his stomach. "What the hell was that for?"

"For not returning one of my damn letters, you stupid fucker."

It was true. Harper had written him a letter a week while he was inside. He had read them. Every word. She'd been very careful to include little hints about what he really wanted to know about—or who, to be perfectly honest—without giving away too much. Each letter had been designed to entice him to ask her for more information.

He never did.

What was the point of asking about Mischa? She obviously didn't want to know how he was doing. After he'd turned her, she'd pushed him away about as far and as fast as possible. For once, he'd let her. Now they were so far apart, he knew it'd be nearly impossible for them to find their way back to one another. Time to accept that and move on.

"I'm sorry about not returning your letters, Harper."

She snorted, unlocking the passenger door for him before making her way around the car and settling into the driver's seat. "Whatever."

He watched, half *be*mused and half *a*mused as she waged war with her seatbelt, which didn't seem to want to stretch over the full girth of her stomach. After a full minute of cursing, grunting, and wiggling in her seat, she managed to beat the offending seatbelt into submission and started the car.

She blew a curl off her forehead and shot him a dark look out of the corner of her eye. "Laugh and I'll stake you."

He swallowed a smile. "Wouldn't dream of it."

She stayed quiet for a full five minutes as they drove— which he imagined was a personal best for Harper—before she blurted out,

"Aren't you even curious how she's doing?"

He sighed. Curious didn't even begin to cover it. Letting her go had cost him a piece of whatever soul he had left after all the centuries he'd been stalking the earth. Not that it mattered. He couldn't force her to love him the way he loved her.

"I'm sure you're taking good care of her," he said mildly.

Harper grumbled under her breath about stubborn dumbasses and relationship-phobes before saying, "Of course I am. We all are. But that's hardly the point. Do you even *know* what the point is?"

She paused long enough for him to mutter, "No, but I'm sure you'll tell me."

Harper didn't miss a beat. "The point is that she struggles every damn day with what she is and how to function as a vampire. You know she blacked out the whole city during *The Walking Dead*, right? Someone cut her off in traffic, she got frustrated, lost control of her power, and I missed the season finale."

How Harper had managed to make this about her, he had no idea, but his stomach churned at the thought of Mischa struggling to accept what she'd become. It hadn't occurred to him that he'd transfer any of his powers to her, either. Damn it. No wonder she hated him.

"She's letting the neighbor keep her dog—and she loves that fucking dog—because she's afraid she'll hurt the damn thing in some of bloodlust stupor, and I even caught her researching vampire power suppressants online one time."

He stiffened. That shit wasn't anything to joke about. The government only used vampire power suppressants with the most dangerous vampires when no other options were available. The side effects of such drugs were too unpredictable. Too deadly.

Besides, a vampire's powers were…elemental. Part of the fabric that held them together. If she couldn't accept what she was and learn to integrate her powers into her life, she'd eventually go mad.

"And even though she has me and Riddick and Leon and Benny

and Dr. Vi," she went on, "She doesn't have anyone who really *gets* her, you know?"

She sniffled and swiped a hand under her nose impatiently. "It's just sad that you two can't forget the past and start fresh."

He glanced over at Harper as a horrible realization dawned. "You're not…crying, are you?"

Harper shook her head, but her trembling lower lip and shiny eyes gave her away. "Shit," he grumbled.

"It's fine," she let out on a shaky wail. "The stupid pregnancy hormones make me e-e-emotional sometimes."

Sweet Christ, Harper's moods were a little mercurial on a good day. But with the added hormones? He could only imagine how Riddick must be suffering.

Hunter patted her knee awkwardly. "I'm sorry. It'll be…okay."

She swatted his hand away and shot him a piercing glare. "Don't patronize me. Just tell me you'll talk to Mischa when you get back."

He ran a hand over his prison-issue buzz cut in frustration. Telling her to mind her own business was probably not a good idea, given her current chaotic emotional state. "I'm sorry, but I won't promise you anything."

Harper glanced at him out of the corner of her eye, and the power in even that half glance was a little terrifying. It was a good thing Harper was psychic and not pyrokinetic. If she had fire at her fingertips, he'd be reduced to a pile of ash with that glare of hers.

"Look," she began again, "I know your relationship with Mischa has always been a little…Pepé Le Pew. And I'm sure that's annoying as hell for you."

He blinked. "Pepé Le Pew?"

She made a sweeping hand gesture and said, "Yeah, you know, she runs, you chase."

Pop culture wasn't exactly his forte, and he often had trouble following Harper's train of thought when she threw in random television or movie references, but *that* reference, he was pretty sure he understood. He just couldn't believe she'd *said* it. "Did you just compare me to a cartoon skunk?"

"Well, you're certainly not the little cat with the wet paint stripe down her back," she said, her tone positively dripping with *well duh*.

Pregnancy had made this woman genuinely crazy. There was no other explanation for it. "What's your point?"

"My point is that while I know Mischa can be infuriating, we both know you love her, and she loves you. Just don't shut the door on the possibility that you'll both grow up and work things out."

He chose to ignore the "grow up" part. "And what makes you so sure she has any interest in working things out with me?"

She snorted. "Hello? Psychic, remember?"

Why did he feel like her assertions had more to do with her desire to bend all people and situations to her will, and less to do with any real feelings Mischa might still have for him?

"You know," he began carefully, "you can't *always* get your way. At some point, things will not go your way, and there won't be anything you can do about it."

Harper laughed out loud at that. "Not bloody likely, my friend. Haven't you heard? I'm semi-charmed."

Semi-charmed, fully crazy, completely hormonal, and least partly Machiavellian, by Hunter's estimation.

He shook his head. "You're a frightening woman, Harper Hall."

She grinned at him. "If everyone could just remember that right up front, we'd all save *so* much time."

Chapter Five

"You gotta pop your cherry sometime, hotness."

Mischa tossed back a glass full of synthetic type O and grimaced, barely resisting the urge to spit it out on the bar and claw it off her tongue with her fingers. She glared over at Benny, who'd insisted they go out for a drink after work. Her instincts had told her to say no.

Thanks for the advice, Vi, she thought sourly.

"I've asked you repeatedly not to call me that," she reminded him. "And if you ever refer to me biting a human as 'popping my cherry' again, I'll rip your arm off and shove it up your ass."

He grinned at her before downing his Bloody Juan, a mix of cheap tequila and pig's blood. "Feisty. Feisty is super-hot on you. But Harper told you to play nice, remember?" He waggled a finger in her face. "So, no threatening your boss."

Wreck Harper's TV night by accidently losing control of your vampire powers one time and she makes you report to Benny Scarpelli.

So. Not. Fair.

Thank God she'd only interrupted *The Walking Dead*. If her little powers malfunction had ruined *Game of Thrones* night, she'd probably be reporting to Fernando, the janitor, right about now.

"You can't keep living off the bottled stuff, hotness," he went on. "It's not good for you." He grimaced. "And it tastes like feet."

Benny didn't understand her desire to hang onto the last bastion of her humanity. She imagined not many vampires would.

Benny set his drink down on the bar and glanced over his shoulder at the writhing crowd of dancers behind them. He bobbed his head in time to the pounding techno beat that was making Mischa consider stabbing a pencil through her eardrums just to make it stop.

"Come on," he cajoled. "There's at least twenty humans here who'd love nothing more than for you to take a bite out of them."

There were probably more than that in this shithole, she thought.

The Lair was the only vampire-owned club in Whispering Hope, other than the all-male review downtown, of course. But despite the fact that they served blood of all types and kept the place at a very vampire-friendly seventy-eight degrees at all times, actual vampires tended to avoid the place.

And why, one might wonder, would vampires refuse to patronize a club so obviously designed with their comfort in mind?

Just then, a buffoon with a set of plastic fangs and a cape—a fucking *cape*, for Christ's sake—dropped to one knee in front of Mischa and extended a hand to her like Romeo getting ready to sweet-talk Juliet out of her corset.

"I beseech you, my Queen of the Night," he began in a voice better suited to a high school rendition of *Death of a Salesman* than it was to addressing an actual woman, "Take my blood. Make me yours. I will serve you for all eternity."

Mischa closed her eyes and pinched the bridge of her nose as Benny snickered beside her. *This* was why no self-respecting vampire ever showed her face at The Lair.

Goddamn pathetic wannabes.

And just how the hell did they always manage to pick her out of the crowd? It wasn't like her jeans, Ramones T-shirt, and Keds screamed "I'm a vampire." The place was dark enough that no one could really tell what she was drinking, so that couldn't have given her away. Did she have a fucking sign on her back or something?

After taking a moment to compose herself—or in reality, gathering enough strength to avoid throat-chopping the irritating little toad—Mischa met his hopeful stare and looked down her nose at him.

"Get up. Turn around, go home, and never come here again. You're lucky to be human."

His brown eyes glazed over for a moment, and without a word, he stood up and shuffled out the door.

She stared at his retreating form, confused.

She turned back around to find Benny staring at her with a speculative look in his eye that made her nervous. "What just happened?" she asked.

He shook his head. "Not sure, but I think you just mind-fucked him and made him your bitch."

Mischa rubbed her temples. "I didn't mean to. I was just making a suggestion." A really, *really* strong suggestion, apparently.

"I don't see the problem, hotness. You're lucky. It usually takes centuries for vamps to develop those kind of skills. Halfers never have any super powers." He snapped his fingers. "Hey, I have a few parking tickets. Think you could, you know," he paused, wiggling his nose like Samantha on *Bewitched*, "make with the vampire magic and clear that shit up for me?"

She shot him a glare instead of kicking him in the shins like her instinct told her to.

Again, thanks a lot, Vi. The kick would've been *so* much more satisfying.

Benny cleared his throat and glanced away. "I'll take that as a *no*."

What everyone failed to realize was that her *powers* were more often than not just freak luck and usually didn't work out *at all* as she'd intended. She just as easily could've given the guy a suggestion and had it totally backfire on her. She could've told him to go away and had him instead start serenading her in Italian while attempting to dry-hump her leg.

Yeah, that'd happened. She still couldn't show her face in Costco, for God's sake.

She sighed, suddenly exhausted. "What are we doing here, Benny? I should probably get back to the office and fill out my expense reports."

He shifted his gaze away from hers, looking decidedly uncomfortable. "Harper thought maybe you'd want to be somewhere that wasn't, uh, the office tonight."

She didn't ask why. The wrenching pain that instantly hit her gut told her everything she needed to know.

Hunter was being released tonight.

Hunter had lived in the basement apartment in the building that housed Harper Hall Investigations for about seven years. She imagined Harper was planning to pick him up at the prison and bring him home. Her friend probably assumed—rightfully assumed—that having Mischa in the building when he came home would be weird. Painful.

Like having her heart ripped out through her nose.

So while she was mentally grousing about having to report to Benny (and threatening him with bodily harm), he was hanging out with her (when he more than likely had much better things to do), just to keep her from hurting all alone.

Well, that settled it. She was officially the biggest bitch in the world.

Mischa swallowed her pride and glanced over at him. "Thank you."

Benny cupped a hand around his ear and leaned toward her, giving her a playful smirk. "What was that you whispered ever-so-faintly, hotness? That thing you said that was so quiet not even a dude with supernatural hearing could hear?"

She fought down a chuckle and looked away. "I said thank you, Benny."

His gaze shot to the ceiling and he threw his arms out dramatically. "Is this the end? Is the sky falling? Surely fire and brimstone are raining down from heaven if *Mischa Bartone* is apologizing to little ol' *me*. What's next? You admitting that you actually *like* me and that we're *friends*?"

Mischa didn't have any friends other than Harper and Vi. And that was only because they'd bullied their way into her life and heart.

Caring only gets you hurt.

It was a truth she'd lived by her whole life. It'd kept her safe and whole on more than one occasion.

But you're not alive anymore. Why not give a new motto a try? Do the opposite of what your instinct tells you to do.

Mischa frowned. It was a little disconcerting to hear Violet's voice in her thoughts.

So with a sigh, she turned to Benny and said, "You know, Benny, I could use a friend right about now. Thanks."

Benny's jaw dropped comically. "Shit, are you serious? You must be in worse shape than Harper thought if you're considering bein' my friend."

She couldn't help but smile. "Maybe. Think my judgment is questionable?"

He tipped his head to the side and considered her for a moment. "Hmmm. I dunno. Wanna make out?"

"Blech! No way. What's the matter with you?"

Benny grinned and threw an arm around her shoulders. "Good news, hotness. Your judgment is fine. And," he paused for dramatic effect, "you have yourself a new friend."

Chapter Six

About an hour and six Bloody Juans later, Benny got a call from Angela, who was apparently ready to forgive him for his "butt stuff" request. In response, Mischa's new friend dumped her at Harper Hall Investigations and lit out of there like his ass was on fire.

Mischa smiled, a little surprised to realize she was actually happy for the lovable little loser.

Maybe Vi's advice was paying off, after all.

She grabbed a file of receipts off her desk, deciding she'd work on her expense reports at home, and locked the door behind her.

Rounding the corner, heading to her car, she ran face-first into a brick wall. She would've fallen on her ass if the brick wall hadn't reached out and latched onto her arm, steadying her.

Mischa's brain eventually caught up to the rest of her senses and she realized it wasn't a wall she'd run into, but a man. She didn't even really have to look at him. The knot in her stomach told her exactly who he was.

Her gaze moved up over muscular legs encased in battered, faded denim, to a wrinkled black t-shirt stretched across his chest—the same chest she'd laid her head on the last time she'd gotten a full eight hours of sleep.

She sniffed delicately. There were stains on his shirt. Blood. Her blood and his.

He was wearing the same clothes he'd been in the night she died. The night he'd been carted off to prison. The night he'd taken three bullets to the back trying to shield her.

The night she let him think she hated him.

Reaching down deep for courage, she looked up—way, way the hell up, because she was so short she only came up to his shoulder—and his melted-chocolate brown eyes stared right back at her.

His hair was different. The shampoo-commercial shiny ebony locks that had reached down to just below his shoulders had been shorn in a prison buzz cut. She'd always loved his long hair, but this new cut hid nothing—not the creamy perfection of his caramel-colored skin, not the knife-edged cheekbones typical of his Lakota heritage, not the intensity in his eyes—and gave him a sharper, harder look.

He looked...dangerous. Lethal. Like the most beautiful predator she'd ever seen.

But most importantly, he was *here*. Right in front of her. He was beautiful and perfect and *here*...and she was staring up at him, speechless, like a dumbass. Quite possibly with drool on her chin.

Then she noticed the angry gash snaking across his cheekbone. Without thinking, she raised her hand toward his face. "What—"

He jerked back as if she'd taken a swing at him, letting go of her arm so quickly she stumbled back a few steps.

When Hunter had been shot on their last night together, two of the bullets ripped through his flesh and into hers. She'd taken one bullet to the throat, and another to the chest. And neither of those bullets hurt half as much as watching Hunter's eyes go cold as he moved away from her.

And the worst part? She deserved that cold stare. She deserved his rejection.

"Hunter," she said, voice raspy, "I'm so—"

She trailed off as he turned and stalked away without a word.

Beside her, Harper huffed out an exasperated sigh. "Well, that didn't go *at all* as I had it planned in my head."

Mischa blinked back tears. (Yes, vampires cry. They cry blood instead of salt water, but still...) "How did it go in your head?"

"Kinda like that Hallmark Channel movie we made fun of at

Christmas time?"

Mischa let out a bitter laugh. Yeah, there probably weren't any dramatic declarations of love and marriage proposals in her immediate future.

But Harper, true to form, slung an arm around her shoulders and said the one thing she knew could help at a time like this. "I'll be your designated driver. Want to get trashed?"

She rested her head on Harper's shoulder. "God yes."

Chapter Seven

Violet downed her fifth shot and laid her cheek on the bar, knocking her glasses askew. "I worked with that damned werewolf for eight years—*eight years*—and tried every legit psychological tactic in the book to get him to quit peeing in the house to mark his territory. I even tried hypnosis, for God's sake. You know what his wife tried that eventually worked?"

Harper popped a greasy, fried ball of cheese, potatoes and jalapenos in her mouth and leaned forward, fascinated. "No, what?"

"A swat on the nose with a rolled up newspaper." Violet crinkled her nose, disgusted. "Eight years of therapy and she cured him with something she probably learned from the *Dog Whisperer*."

Mischa downed her—Jesus, was it the tenth?—shot and glared at Vi. "How does that qualify you as having the worst day ever? Hunter wouldn't even speak to me. He pulled away from me like I was a fucking leopard."

Wait, that didn't sound right. And was it her imagination, or did she just slur that whole sentence?

"I'm sure you mean *leper*," Harper said dryly. "Although I'm sure he'd pull away from a leopard, too."

Vi ignored Harper and lifted her head to glare at Mischa, the intensity of her expression marred only by the pretzel stuck to her cheek, and the fact that her icy blond hair—usually coifed to perfection—was standing up in several different directions. "Why do we always have to talk about you, huh?"

"Because you're my sera...serap...therapus..." She gave her head a hard shake. By God, that was a hard word. Why had she never noticed what a hard word that was before? "Because you're my shrink!" she spit out, proud to have found an alternate word for therapist.

Vi looked confused for a minute before throwing her hands up. "Oh, sure, bring *that* up. That's just like you, you know."

Mischa rolled her eyes and almost fell off her bar stool as her body seemed to follow the movement. Harper grabbed her arm and gave her a shove back in the right direction.

"Thank you," Mischa slurred. "I love you."

"I love you, too, Harper," Vi said, leaning over to rest her head on Harper's shoulder. "I mean, I don't really know you, but you're sooooo nice."

Harper snorted and shrugged her off. "Jesus, you two are pathetic drunks."

Vi rubbed a hand over her eyes, seemingly forgetting that she was wearing glasses, and blinked at her surroundings. "What is this place? It's disgusting."

Mischa agreed. The Rag Tag was probably the seediest bar in Whispering Hope. It catered to the city's don't-ask-don't-tell paranormal community. Thieves, con artists, violent criminals…the place was lousy with them every night. She'd collared more than thirty paranormal bail jumpers right at this very bar. Not exactly your typical girls' night out locale.

Harper nodded to her plate of food. "Cheesy tots. It's the only place in town to get them. Tiny makes them special for me." She offered a little finger wave to the three-hundred-pound gorilla of a man polishing glasses behind the bar. He waved back and grinned, displaying a disturbing lack of front teeth.

Vi cringed, then shrugged. "S'all good." She swiveled on her stool and grabbed Mischa's arm. "Hey! You should totally call Hunter and tell him you're sorry. Maybe he'll listen now."

"Yeah, because drunk dialing is always a good idea," Harper said dispassionately, tucking into her cheesy tots again.

Mischa ignored her. "Do you really think he would?"

Vi nodded with enough enthusiasm that Harper had to grab her and right her before she slipped off her stool. "Of course he would! Why wouldn't he? You're awesome." She reached over and patted Mischa's head. "And you have such pretty hair."

"Jesus," Harper muttered.

"Thank you," Mischa said with a sniffle. "You really are a good friend, Vi. And you're a really good terapus…theratis…shrink. I'm sorry I called you a low-rent Dr. Phil."

"You never called me that."

"Of course I didn't." To Harper, she added in a ridiculously loud stage whisper, "Not to her face, anyway."

Harper shook her head and took out her phone.

"Are you calling Hunter?" Vi asked. "Tell him Mischa loves him, and he should love her, because she deserves to be happy and…" she trailed off, frowning. "Am I talking *really* loud?"

"Yes, you are. And no, I'm not calling Hunter. I'm calling Riddick," Harper said. "I'm going to need help pouring you two into a cab."

Mischa's laugh ended in a snort. "Pouring. 'Cause we're drunk. See what she did there? I told you she was sooooo funny."

Vi and Mischa laughed until they slumped over on one another.

They were still laughing when Riddick came in and slid an arm around Harper. "Sunshine," he murmured before leaning over and kissing her like he wanted to devour her, and damn anyone who might be watching.

Mischa sighed and leaned forward, resting her chin on her palm. "You guys are so cute together I want to vomit."

Harper ignored her. Instead, she turned to Vi. "Riddick, this is Mischa's *therapist…*" she said, very carefully enunciating the word, the show-off, "…Dr. Violet Marchand. Vi, this is my husband, Noah Riddick."

Riddick reached out and shook her hand. Vi stared up at him, completely awestruck.

"Holy shit," she eventually whispered. "You're so hot it makes my ovaries hurt."

Riddick's brow furrowed as Vi slapped a hand over her mouth. "Jesus, did I say that out loud?"

Harper nodded, looking amused. "And not in your inside voice, either, Vi."

Mischa could understand Vi's outburst. Riddick was ridiculously good-looking, with his icy blue eyes, olive skin, and longish, sexily disheveled black hair. He was no Hunter, but then again, who was? As far as mere mortals went, Riddick was about as high up on the food chain as a body could get.

"I'm so sorry," Vi mumbled, lowering her forehead to her palm. "I get really nervous around hot guys and any control I have over the filter between my brain and mouth flies right out the window."

Unfortunately, on the word "flies," Vi flung her arms out and smacked Mischa in the face, knocking her right off her bar stool.

As Mischa hoped the liquid she was now lying in was beer and not biohazard, Riddick pulled her to her feet and bent down to look her in the eyes (he had to bend down because he was about a foot taller than her, too, she thought a little bitterly). He frowned.

"How long has she been like this?" Riddick asked Harper.

"Um, maybe an hour or so?"

His frown intensified. "That's not right. Vampires shouldn't stay drunk for that long."

Harper turned to Vi, who'd laid her head back down on the bar and was mumbling something about her sore ovaries under her breath. "Vi, what's wrong with Mischa?"

"Fear of abandonment, rejection. Feelings of self-loathing and low self-esteem." Vi sighed. "She's all twisted and fucked up."

Mischa shook her head and sagged a bit in Riddick's grasp. "I'm fine. I can take care of myself."

Harper scowled at her. "I'd feel better about that if you hadn't just said, 'I can take care of my *shelf*."

She opened her mouth to argue, but all that came out was "Nuh."

Riddick shook his head. "That's not right," he repeated. "I've never seen pupils doing what hers are doing right now."

Harper slid off her barstool and grabbed her phone. "Should I call an ambulance?"

Mischa wanted to say that no, they should most certainly not call an ambulance because she'd had a few too many. How humiliating would that be? But she was all of a sudden so…tired. Maybe if she just closed her eyes for a minute…

"Oh, no you don't," Riddick grumbled, giving her a hard shake. "Wake up!"

Her eyes jerked open. "I was just trying to rest my eyes. Don't be a dick," she slurred.

"Uh huh. Call me whatever you want, just stay awake." He glanced over at Harper, who was shifting her phone nervously from one hand to the other.

"I don't think the hospital can do much for her," he said. "The closest one is Whispering Hope General, and they don't even have a vampire unit."

And why would they? Mischa thought. So few things could damage a vampire that it was hardly worth the cost of the space and personnel.

Harper set her phone down and grabbed Mischa's face with both hands. "Listen to me carefully," she said, slowly, deliberately. "If you die on me again, I will follow you all the way to heaven—or hell—and drag you back. Then I will kill you myself. Do you understand me?"

She didn't. She really didn't. That just didn't make any sense at all. But she sounded super-serious, and usually with Harper, agreement was the best course of action, so she nodded.

"Good," Harper said, scooping up her phone again. "And you're going to just have to forgive me for what I'm about to do."

"What...?"

Harper looked her right in the eye as she spoke into the phone words that terrified and thrilled Mischa in equal measure.

"Hunter, I need your help."

Chapter Eight

It had taken three different soaps and twenty minutes in a scalding hot shower to rid himself of the prison stench he'd stewed in for the length of his stay at Midvale. The clothes he'd been wearing were a complete loss. He'd tossed them into the building's incinerator almost immediately.

Any plans of sleeping in a bed with an actual mattress instead of a wall-mounted slab of steel went out the window when Harper called.

I need your help, she'd said. And like a fool, he'd rushed out the door without even bothering to ask any questions.

He caught the scent as soon as he walked into the bar. It was a scent he'd know anywhere, a scent he could track across continents if necessary.

Mischa.

He followed the scent of cherry bark and almond shampoo layered over lime and coconut hand cream, layered over soft female skin. She always smelled edible. And like she was...

Mine.

It had taken every bit of restraint he had to not fall at her feet earlier. To beg her to give him another chance. To pull her into his arms and never let go. To be Pepé Le Pew and damn the consequences.

Somehow, she was even more beautiful than he remembered, and that was saying a lot, since he'd pretty much built her beauty up in his head to goddess-level proportions while he'd been inside. The almond-shaped, sultry, cocoa-brown eyes, the delicate features she'd inherited from her Italian mother, and the hair...

Jesus. The need to tangle his fingers in those soft, loose, chestnut curls that trailed halfway down her back was damn near crippling.

If he hadn't walked away when he did, he would've embarrassed himself by professing his undying love or some such shit, likely scaring her away again. Just like that damn cartoon skunk.

Harper grabbed his arm when she saw him and dragged him through a crowd of halfers, weres, and vampires—fuck, what were they doing *here*, of all places? They were lucky they hadn't been eaten—to the bar, where he saw Riddick holding Mischa in his arms.

His logical brain knew that Riddick loved his wife, and that he would rather die than disrespect or cheat on Harper. But Hunter's vampire instincts? Yeah, those instincts were pretty much telling him to tear Riddick apart for daring to touch Mischa.

Mine.

Riddick glanced at him. "Thank God you're here."

And with that, Riddick unceremoniously thrust a limp Mischa into his arms.

He had to shift his hold because she wasn't really doing much to support herself, and he finally managed to slide his hands under her arms and haul her up against his chest so that she didn't melt to the floor in a boneless heap.

She surprised him by gripping the edges of his battered army jacket in two white-knuckled fists. Slowly, she lifted her head, her eyes touching on his chest first, then his throat and chin, and finally, her gaze found his. She smiled a tiny, tired smile.

He thought his heart actually might start beating again. So, so beautiful.

"Hi," she whispered.

He didn't respond. If he stopped concentrating on not kissing her so that he could respond…well, he wouldn't be able to *not* kiss her.

That's when he noticed her pupils seemed to be doing some sort of samba. He swore. "When was the last time you fed?"

She blinked up at him, smile fading. "Um…"

Harper said, "Benny took her out a few hours ago. He said she drank some bottled blood then."

He shook his head, still locked in the tractor beam of Mischa's eyes. "No, not the bottled shit. Actual blood."

A little blond with her head down on the bar said, "She's never had actual blood. She's all twisted and fucked up."

That got his attention, and pissed him off pretty good. What the fuck made some drunk at a bar qualified to judge whether or not Mischa was twisted and fucked up?

Harper cleared her throat. "That's Vi. *Dr.* Violet Marchand. She's Mischa's therapist."

Oh. Well…all right then. Maybe she was qualified after all.

The doctor raised her head off the bar regally. Or, at least, it would've been regal if she didn't have mascara smeared on her forehead and a pretzel stuck to her cheek. But minus those minor details, Mischa's doctor looked like a pint-sized Grace Kelly.

She thrust a hand out in his general direction. "It's a pleasure to meet…"

Her sentence trailed off into an inarticulate squeak as she looked up and saw Hunter for the first time. She pulled her hand back slowly and tucked it between her knees. "Sweet merciful crap, they're everywhere," she whispered.

"Oh, pull yourself together, Vi," Harper grumbled. "Yes, he's hot, too. We get it. There's no time for drool; this is a crisis!"

Vi mumbled an apology and laid her head back down on the bar.

Mischa's forehead dropped to his chest. "Hmmm," she murmured, rubbing her cheek on his chest like a sleepy kitten. He went from zero to hard in approximately half a second.

He was *so* damned pathetic.

All right, enough was enough. Adjusting his hold yet again, he scooped her up and held her against his chest. "I'll take care of her," he said to Harper. He nodded to Riddick. "Can you get these two home?"

"Yeah," Riddick said, laying a hand on Violet's shoulder. "Come on, doc, time to go."

Vi's only response came in the form of a snuffling snore.

"Fucking perfect," Riddick muttered.

In one smooth motion, Riddick chucked an unconscious Vi over his shoulder, took Harper's hand, and started moving toward the door. Mischa lifted her head in time to watch them go.

"You're not taking me to the hospital, are you?" she asked.

Hunter shifted her so that he could fish her keys out of her pocket. They'd have to take her car. He'd walked here (well, ran, really), and while he could carry her for miles, he knew she'd probably be more comfortable in a car. "No. They can't help you. I can."

She shivered. "Where are you taking me, then?"

The one place he knew he shouldn't, which also happened to be the place he'd wanted to take her ever since they first met over two decades ago.

"Home, Mischa. I'm taking you home."

Chapter Nine
1992, Sentry Headquarters

Hunter glared down at the name on the slip of paper he'd taken from the dead man. Mischa Bartone. The same damn Mischa Bartone who'd ordered nine slayers to kill him over the past year. Ten, if he counted the one whose blood still stained his hands.

He didn't *want* to kill her, but he would. Something told him he'd never again know a moment's peace unless he choked the life out of her. She obviously didn't give up easily.

Not bothering to hide from the security cameras, he walked right past no fewer than twelve guards at the main gate, and three inside the building. Weak-minded, all of them. One simple telepathic push and they'd all looked the other way as he strolled in as if he belonged there. And in truth, no one belonged there *less* than he did.

Hunter didn't have to trail her scent—a fruity mixture—for long before he found her office. He didn't bother knocking. The door burst off its hinges with one well-placed kick.

The woman standing behind the desk was...unexpected.

She was tiny. Standing on tiptoe, she probably didn't reach five-foot-three, and she couldn't weigh more than 110 pounds. The biggest thing about her was the mass of chestnut curls that fell to the middle of her back.

She had almond-shaped, melted-chocolate eyes hiding behind wire-rimmed glasses and golden skin that hinted at Italian heritage. Her features were delicate, complete with full, pouty lips, high cheekbones, and a pointy little chin.

That pointy little chin took on a defiant tilt as she stared back at him, looking insultingly unruffled. Obviously, she wasn't going to give him the satisfaction of hearing her speak first.

"You can't be..." he began.

One delicate black brow winged up. "I'm Mischa Bartone. I'm quite sure I'm the one you're looking for."

Not possible. "But you're…"

"A woman?" she supplied.

The most beautiful woman I've ever seen. "You're a child."

She frowned. "How did you find me?"

He tossed her the note. "I tracked your scent off this."

She looked a bit nonplussed by that. At least he'd gotten some emotion out of her. She'd seemed fairly bored up until that point.

"If you're waiting for an invitation, you won't be getting one."

He liked her voice. It was smooth and rich and low-pitched, yet utterly feminine. "What makes you think I need one?"

"Vampires 101. You can't come in uninvited."

"You've received misinformation, I'm afraid, Miss Bartone. Quite a bit of it."

Her eyes narrowed. "Really? What misinformation might that be?"

"You and your superiors seem to think I'm in the habit of killing humans. That hasn't been a hobby of mine for over a century."

Her lip curled at the word *hobby*. "I have nine dead slayers that might argue that point."

He pulled the dog tags he'd taken from the dead man out of his coat pocket and tossed them to her. She caught them without taking her eyes off him.

"You have *ten* dead slayers, Miss Bartone," he said. "And I wouldn't have killed any of them if given any other choice."

He heard her gulp, but her expression remained emotionless. "Congratulations, Wolf Hunter. Ten slayers. That must be some kind of record."

He growled as she dropped gracefully into her chair. "It's *just* Hunter."

The name Wolf Hunter, the rough English translation of his

actual name, had been fine back in 1492 in Lakota territory, but these days, it made him sound like a Calvin Klein underwear model or struggling metal singer. "And I'm not here to brag," he snapped. "I'm here to tell you to stop sending slayers after me."

"I'm only doing my job."

"And I'm only doing mine."

She stared at him for a moment, then her gaze dropped. After a moment, she said, "Can I ask you a question?"

The righteous indignation had bled from her voice and she sounded so...young. Sad. He steeled himself against feeling sympathy for the woman who'd ordered his death. Ten times. "I suppose so."

"Was it..." she paused, catching her full lower lip between her teeth. The sight did things to his libido he wasn't proud of. "...Did any of them even present a challenge to you?"

"You mean did any of them even come close to being able to kill me?"

She nodded, curls bobbing.

No one had ever asked him about the full extent of his powers. He imagined she wouldn't be standing there so calmly if she knew what he could do. He sighed.

"Miss Bartone, I've been around a very long time. I've fought in so many wars I probably can't even remember all of them. I have more training and experience than all of your slayers put together."

He paused before adding, "So, to answer your question, no, none of them were even able to hurt me. And to answer what you *really* want to know, yes, I'll keep killing the men you send after me, one by one. My existence isn't ideal, but I intend to protect it nonetheless."

Her gaze turned speculative. After a few moments, she groaned. "All I can do is make a recommendation to my superiors to stop sending people after you. I can't guarantee they'll take it."

Hunter was over five hundred years-old. Nothing had surprised him in, well, centuries, he supposed. And yet Mischa Bartone, this tiny little slip of a girl, had just managed to shock the hell out of him.

"You'd do that?"

That defiant chin came up again. "Well, I certainly would rather have you killed, per my orders," she said, voice prim. "But since it doesn't look like that's going to happen anytime soon, a truce certainly seems to be in my team's best interest."

He resisted the urge to snort. "Truce, huh? I've heard that before."

She rolled her eyes. "Oh, please. If you bring up George Custer, the whole deal's off. I'm not going to be held accountable for mistakes made hundreds of years ago."

He couldn't hold back his sharp bark of laughter. She'd never know how close to the truth her Custer statement was. "Fair enough."

He let his gaze roam the length of her. For such a tiny thing, she certainly wasn't lacking for curves. "You know, Miss Bartone, under a different set of circumstances, you and I could have been…"

She straightened to her full height, which still only put the top of her head at the level of his breastbone. "Don't even think it," she said through visibly clenched teeth.

Interesting. She was even more stunning when she was angry.

Admittedly, he didn't know much about the specifics of her job. He knew watchers dispatched slayers, followed orders from Sentry leadership, and, well, watched what happened. But she didn't look like she fit into the standard watcher mold. She obviously didn't blindly follow her orders. She was an anomaly. A puzzle. And if there was one thing he couldn't abide, it was an unsolved puzzle.

He titled his head to one side as he studied her. "You don't look like any of the other watchers."

Her frown suggested she'd heard that comment before. "You were expecting someone older? Taller, maybe?"

"I was expecting someone less beautiful."

Her cheeks flushed red. "Flatter me all you want, I'm still not inviting you in."

He chuckled. "You're still so sure I need an invitation?"

"I think you would've killed me already if you didn't."

"I didn't come here to kill you." At least, he'd *hoped* he wouldn't have to.

Her expression gave nothing away, so he dropped his guard telepathically, hoping to catch a few of her stray thoughts.

Sure you didn't. I fucking hate liars.

Well, she'd managed to shock him yet again. "I have no reason to lie to you." And just to throw her off her game—which was admittedly better than his own—he added, "And what an unladylike turn of phrase."

Bingo. Apparently Miss Bartone hadn't been aware that centuries-old vampires often had certain...talents that younger vampires lacked. Her eyes widened and her mouth fell open.

But true to form, she regained her composure quickly. "You're not invited into my head either, *Hunter*, so stay out of it."

A chill—and not the bad kind—skated down his spine as he leaned against her doorjamb. "I enjoy hearing my name on your lips."

A commotion down the hall (rattling keys and squeaky sneakers on the cheap vinyl flooring, mostly) kept him from hearing her next thought.

"Security knows you're here," she said. "You'd better go or else our little deal's off."

He winked at her. "They won't even know I'm here."

Her skepticism was clear as she crossed her arms over her chest and watched him, silently.

A security guard—Curtis, his nametag read—raced around the corner and yelled, "Freeze!"

Hunter glanced at the .22 Curtis was pointing at his chest. Getting shot with it at close range would do little more than annoy him. "You missed the intruder," he said, pitching his voice an octave lower than usual. "He's long gone. You'll want to disable the alarm now."

He looked back at Mischa and smirked at her slack jaw and

widened eyes. Curtis' expression went completely blank. "Sorry to disturb your work, Miss Bartone," he said, voice devoid of any emotion or tone. "The intruder is long gone. I'll just go disable the alarm now."

No wonder my slayers hadn't stood a chance against him. He probably convinced them to kill themselves! Wait a minute...

"You son of a bitch," she hissed. "Did you use mind control on me to—"

He raised a hand in supplication. "No. The truce truly was your idea. The extremely stubborn and strong-willed seem to be immune to mind control," he added pointedly.

And then it was like a black curtain fell over her thoughts. Amazing. Not many humans could block his telepathy. She was a surprise indeed.

"I think you need to go now before I decide the truce isn't such a wise idea after all," she said, glaring at him over the top of her glasses.

He smiled. He couldn't help it. Then he felt the mental wall she'd erected crumble a bit around the edges, allowing him to pick up her thoughts again.

With a smile like that, he just might be able to exert some control over me.

If his heart still beat, it would've skipped at that point.

"Now *that* is truly good to know," he murmured a moment before he grabbed her wrist, yanked her into the hall and pressed his lips to hers, quick and firm.

She was going to push him away. He could sense it. His disappointment was surprisingly crushing, given he'd only just met her.

He regretfully pulled away and disappeared on her at a pace he knew the human eye couldn't follow. He'd just reached the outer gate of the compound when he heard her shout, "Truce is off, you asshole. If I ever see you again, I'll kill you myself!"

Hunter laughed out loud. "We'll see, love. We'll see."

Chapter Ten

Hunter sat down on the edge of the bed beside Mischa, wet washcloth in hand.

Her eyes opened and fell on him, a little glazed. Her brow furrowed. "Am I dead?"

He raised a brow and wiped her forehead, hoping the cool water would help her regain a bit of her focus. "Technically, yes, you are."

A ghost of a smile played about her lips. "Yeah, I guess I am. I guess I mean…am I dreaming? Is this real?"

She looked so hopeful and trusting lying there. In his bed. Where she belonged.

He gave himself a sharp mental slap across the face. *Don't go down that rabbit hole again.* "You need blood," he said bluntly. "Not the bottled crap. Actual blood."

A frown line creased her smooth brow. "The bottled blood has all the—"

"Yeah, yeah, I know," he interrupted. "The bottled blood has all the nutritional requirements vampires need. I've seen the commercials, too. The fact is you can *mostly* survive on the bottled blood. But when you do something stupid—like getting hurt or *drunk*," he paused for effect, "you'll need real blood to recover."

"That part's not in the commercials," she mumbled.

"No, it's not."

"Do you have bagged blood?"

He'd needed every bag Harper had put in his fridge to recover from the months of starvation in prison. He shook his head. "You'll need to drink from me."

She blinked, obviously struggling to keep up with the conversation. "Are you suggesting that I...feed off you?"

He'd expected her to sound appalled at the idea. She didn't. She sounded...interested. It took every remaining ounce of his restraint to stay out of her thoughts. At this point, he'd give his left nut to know what she was thinking, but at the same time, there was a part of him that knew he was better off wondering.

He gave her a curt nod. "Wrist or throat?"

She tried to sit up and failed, falling back on his pillow with a muttered curse. "Is there really no other way?"

He shrugged. "You could drink bottled blood. Wait this out. You might feel better in a few days. Maybe not."

Her frown line deepened. "A few days? I start a new job for Harper tomorrow."

Yes, her job. Chasing down bail-jumping, dangerous vampires. He couldn't express how much he *loathed* the idea of her putting herself in danger like that.

But she wasn't his to protect anymore. Not that she would've listened to him even if she was.

In answer, he offered her his wrist. "You'll feel better in moments."

And he'd be in hell. She had no way of knowing it, but a vampire's bite was pure, unadulterated pleasure. Damn near orgasmic. So while she was simply feeding, he'd be struggling to retain control and not jump her like a rutting beast.

Which, technically, he was kind of doing now anyway, so...maybe he'd really be no worse off.

Fuck, now he was arguing with himself. That couldn't be good for his mental health.

She shot him a skeptical look. "I didn't think vampires could feed from one another."

"They can't. You can feed from me only because I'm your sire. Your blood—your human blood—is a part of me from when I changed you. It will always be part of me."

Just like my stupid, pathetic heart will always be yours.

Her gaze turned serious as she wrapped her slender fingers around his wrist. "Are you sure?"

No. Not at all.

He nodded slowly.

Chapter Eleven

The tiny pop of his skin breaking under the hesitant pressure of her fangs was weirdly...sensual. Her eyes flew to his and she found him watching her, unblinking. A muscle in his jaw jumped as she pulled gently on the wound.

The taste of his blood was heavenly. Like nothing she'd ever tasted. Heat and strength and wild energy...it was unfathomable.

"Harder," he said through clenched teeth. "Take more."

He hissed when she sucked harder. His already dark eyes darkened further, with pain or pleasure, she had no idea. She stopped caring as his blood, which tasted better than any human food she'd ever had, filled her mouth and rolled down her throat.

She'd been a vampire for months, and everything about her had sharpened in that time. Her vision, hearing, strength, and speed improved exponentially. Her skin became smoother, completely unlined, and almost luminescent. Hell, even her hair healed itself, becoming thicker and fuller with not so much as a single split end in sight. But as she continued to take Hunter's blood, she realized the enhancements she'd already experienced were only the beginning.

Suddenly she could hear every heartbeat in the building, as well as a few on the street. And the smells! God, she could smell hot dogs sizzling on a street vendor's rolling grill that was at least half a mile away, the earthy scents of soil and lake water from the park she knew was five miles away. And Hunter's skin...

The scent of his skin under her nose was stronger than she'd ever realized. Spicy and sweet at the same time, and when mingled with her own scent, it was sheer perfection. Orgasmic. He smelled like...

Mine.

With a growl she released his wrist and knocked him flat on his back onto the floor. She crawled on top of him and sank her fangs into his neck.

Vi's advice about working against her instincts fled in the face of this new, almost primal need take what was *hers*.

To take *him*.

He muttered something she didn't quite catch before one of his hands slid into her hair, holding her head at his throat, and his other hand started moving restlessly over her shoulder, her back, before finally coming to rest on her hip.

She groaned, pulling her fangs out of his throat and licking the marks she'd left behind. "Missed you so much," she murmured.

Her hands seemed to move of their own volition, tracing the familiar hard lines and contours of his chest, shoulders, and stomach through the thin cotton of his T-shirt.

He lifted her off him just enough to kiss her, and she slanted her mouth across his, desperate for more of his taste.

Hunter pulled her closer and groaned when she tightened her thighs on his hips.

In the darkest recesses of her mind, something tugged at her. Made her think there was something they should be talking about. But that and all other thought fled as his tongue and breathless moans tangled with hers.

They went to work on each other's clothes with preternatural speed, fabric shredding and tearing in the melee. She shivered at the sheer, unadulterated pleasure of finally, *finally* having his bare skin against hers.

He broke their kiss, moving his hands to her face so that she had to look at him. She moaned at the loss of contact and went for him again, but he held her back.

"If you're going to stop me, do it now."

Her lust-soaked brain didn't understand his words, and it didn't understand his tone. It sounded like a warning and a plea all at the same time.

She licked her lips, tasting him, and his eyes followed the motion. "Don't stop," she choked out. "Please don't stop."

***

Hunter muttered something that could've been a prayer of thanks, or a curse. They shouldn't be doing this. She was half-crazed with the effects of taking real blood straight from a donor for the first time. It was possible she'd regret this as soon as his blood finished burning away the alcohol in hers.

He should say no. Tell her to leave.

She should say no.

But she didn't. She didn't understand. His control was razor-thin, tenuous at best. He'd wanted her for too long to walk away and do the honorable thing.

The first brush of her plump pink lips and fangs on his flesh had been his undoing. But if he was being honest with himself, he knew his fate had been sealed long, long ago. Long before she'd become a vampire.

They'd made love before, when she was human. Tonight would be different. Tonight he didn't have to hold back for fear of hurting her. She was as indestructible as he was. And if her scent and expression of raw, dazed need were any indication, she wanted him as much as he wanted her.

She rocked her hips, rubbing along the hard ridge of his erection, the erection he'd had pretty much since her mouth had touched his. A moan slid from her lips and that was the end of him letting her control the situation.

When he sat up, Mischa growled and tried to hold him down, using her fledgling vampire strength. But Hunter was much, much older and much, much stronger. He easily reversed their position, picked her up and tossed her on the bed, following her down in one smooth motion.

She reared up, but he caught her wrists in one hand and pinned them above her head.

"Now," she said, straining against him, catching his lower lip between her teeth. Her voice lowered and she hissed, "Take me *now*."

He couldn't agree more, but… "Did you just try and use compulsion to make me fuck you?"

Her eyes widened and her mouth fell open. She hadn't even realized she'd done it. That was something they'd need to work on.

Later.

"You won't need compulsion."

There was no time for foreplay. No time for murmured endearments and tenderness. There was only this.

Taking.

Taking what's mine.

With one hard thrust, he drove into her.

He froze above her, his eyes locked on hers.

Oh God oh God oh God. She wanted so badly to move, but couldn't. She was terrified she'd ruin this moment, the moment where nothing they'd been through mattered. There was nothing but the two of them, locked together, exactly where they belonged.

Mine.

The tension in his face was mesmerizing, raw and primal. She clenched her inner muscles around him, and that was apparently all it took to break his control.

His mouth came down on hers in a fierce kiss as he surged forward, sinking deeper into her. She thought she might have cried out, but couldn't be sure. Her entire being was focused on him. On the way his chest slid against the softness of her breasts with every deep thrust. On the way his tongue mated with hers, mimicking the actions of their bodies. On the flex and pull of the muscles rippling under his smooth, taut skin.

It was almost too much. Too intense. More intense than it had ever been between them.

"So wet," he murmured against her collarbone. "So tight. M*ine*."

She gasped as his fangs pierced the skin between her neck and shoulder, and with that, she plummeted over the edge.

She came hard, screaming his name, arching beneath him. She struggled to loosen his hold on her wrists so she could touch him, but he held tight, watching her intently as the seemingly endless waves of her orgasm rode her hard.

But he didn't slow down. Hunter lifted her hips with his free hand so that every deep, long stroke ground against her clitoris. Every stroke was like a brand, proving his earlier declaration.

Mine.

Her second climax hit so hard and fast that she was completely caught off guard. Her entire body clenched, the paroxysm even more powerful than before.

He followed her over the edge a moment later with a primal, guttural sound as she writhed beneath him.

He let go of her wrists and collapsed on top of her. They stayed silent for long moments afterward. Him lying on top of her, deliciously heavy, as she trailed her fingers lightly up and down the muscled planes of his back.

Reality crept back into her sex-soaked brain slowly, but insidiously. They had so much to talk about. So much to set straight. So many wrongs to right. She hadn't even apologized to him yet for her desertion after he turned her.

"Hunter, I—"

"No."

She blinked. *Um, what?* "But I didn't—"

"I said *no*."

And with that, he pulled out of her and flipped her over. She grabbed the edge of the mattress as his weight settled on her again.

"We're not talking right now," he growled in her ear.

She gasped as he slid into her from behind. Her fingers tightened reflexively on the mattress. "Okay," she choked out, helplessly arching her hips back against him. "No talking."

And, as it turned out, he was true to his word. They didn't talk for the next eight hours.

Chapter Twelve

Doing the walk of shame was one thing. But doing the walk of shame, sans underwear, into your place of business? Well, Mischa figured that was probably walk of shame rock-bottom.

Waking up alone was bad enough. Throughout their entire eight hours or so together, the only words she'd exchanged with Hunter were of the "Oh, God, yes, right there, don't stop, harder, harder, faster, more" variety. He wouldn't really allow anything else. Every time she'd tried to talk to him, he'd shifted positions and fucked her to distraction.

Not that she'd minded at the time, of course. But now, she was pretty sure they'd exhausted every position in the *Kama Sutra*, and she was still no closer to apologizing to him, thanks to his disappearing act while she'd fallen into an exhausted, sex-drugged slumber.

She'd waited around for him as long as possible, hoping he'd just stepped out and would return shortly. But after an hour or so, it was clear he was purposefully avoiding her, and she had to get to work.

So, she'd been forced to steal a T-shirt from his closet (her clothes looked like they'd been shredded by a pack of angry badgers) and walk-of-shame it upstairs to Harper Hall Investigations.

"Say nothing," she'd growled as she walked past Benny, Leon and a slack-jawed Harper to get to the bathroom, where she kept an emergency change of clothes.

Her time as a skip-tracer had taught her that any manner of disgusting things could happen to one's clothing when apprehending bail-jumping vampires and shapeshifters, and having a fresh set of clothes handy was always prudent.

Half an hour later, freshly changed and with the stench of humiliation forcibly scrubbed from her skin, she sat with Harper, Benny, and Leon, discussing the case of the missing beauty queens.

"So, Barbie has worked it out with the judges so that you'll make it through every elimination until the winner is chosen. Of course, if we solve this thing before then, you'll be disqualified. I'll make up some cover story for you."

The glitter in Harper's eyes spelled her doom, so Mischa quickly said, "*I get to pick the reason for my disqualification.*"

Harper pouted. "Party pooper."

Better to be called a party pooper than to be publically disqualified for posing for a *smackthatbigass.com* webcam, or for offering to blow the judges, or whatever horrific story Harper came up with. It was always best to never give Harper creative freedom over, well, pretty much anything.

"Anyhoo," Harper went on, "I'll go in with you as your assistant," she made finger quotes on assistant, "to help with your hair and makeup. All the other contestants have an assistant, so it won't seem weird to anyone."

Well, that was a relief since Mischa didn't even own any makeup. If left to her own devices, she'd probably end up looking like Heath Ledger in *The Dark Knight*.

"Barbie assigned Riddick to the lighting crew, which he's *thrilled* about."

Mischa could imagine. The thought of antisocial Riddick in a room with fifty pageant contestants was downright comical.

"So, I think that covers all our bases," Harper said, looking pretty pleased with herself. "I can chat up the other assistants and see if I can pick up any visions, you can chat up the contestants, and Riddick can..." she paused, looking thoughtful, knowing damn well Riddick would never *chat up* anyone, "well, he can threaten the crew into telling him anything he wants to know."

Benny rubbed his hands together and leaned forward in his chair.

"Great. What do I do on this one, Harp?"

She frowned. "First of all, you never call me Harp again. Second, I'll need you to run down any leads any of us get while we're on the inside. You just need to be available to us whenever we call, basically."

Leon snickered. "You're their bitch, in other words." Benny gave him the finger, which Leon ignored. "What do you need me to do, Harper?"

Harper looked him dead in the eye, serious as a heart attack, and said, "You have the most important mission of all."

He puffed up in his chair, shot Benny a snooty glare, and said, "Yeah? What's that?"

"My lunch. I need cheesy tots and a bacon double cheeseburger. Stat."

Benny laughed and it was Leon's turn to give him the finger. Mischa just shook her head, fondly. Sure, there were times when she felt like she was the only adult in the room and it irked the shit out of her, but today wasn't one of them.

Funny what, oh, thirty or forty orgasms can do for a girl's attitude.

Leon clapped his hands together. "Good. Now that business is out of the way, can finally address the elephant in the room?"

There was a pause before Harper deadpanned, "Everyone better quit looking at me or someone's gonna die."

Benny chuckled as Leon rolled his eyes and said, "No. Not *you*. Her!" He pointed at Mischa. "Is no one going to ask why she came in here wearing nothing but a T-shirt and a guilty look?"

Benny and Harper glanced at her, then said, "Nope," in stereo.

Mischa raised a brow at him and smirked.

"Fine," he grumbled. "But if I showed up in nothing but a T-shirt, you'd have questions."

Since Leon lived in his mom's basement and hadn't had a date in, well, ever, as far as Mischa knew, him showing up half naked probably meant someone had rolled him the parking lot.

"Listen, I have a doctor's appointment," Harper said, "so you should have plenty of time to go home and get ready before the contestant welcome meeting. I'll meet you there."

Mischa frowned down at her jeans, black T-shirt, and black leather jacket. "I am ready."

Harper blinked at her, then burst out laughing. "Have you ever seen a beauty pageant? Do you think *Honey Boo Boo* would wear jeans and a T-shirt to orientation?"

Mischa had no idea why her outfit was funny, or who the fuck *Honey Boo Boo* was. It totally sounded like something Harper had made up.

Harper swiped at her watering eyes and said, "No, seriously, you can't wear that. It's *adorable* that you thought you could, though. Stop by my place on the way to the convention center and get my black dress. You can wear that today. Barbie will provide clothes for the rest of the competition."

Mischa pinched the bridge of her nose, praying for strength as she thought about the frilly pink *Cinderella*-looking nightmare Barbie would most certainly have her wearing if given the opportunity.

Guess her panty-less walk of shame into work was really just the tip of her humiliation iceberg.

Awesome.

Chapter Thirteen

Falling asleep during beauty pageant orientation was not the best way to make friends among the contestants.

Mischa would just file that tidbit away under "stuff that would've been good to know about an hour ago."

Honestly, who the hell would've known there were so many rules in a competition like this! No posing for photos outside the competition, not even selfies, until the show aired. No fraternization with the crew. No use of self-tanners, colored contact lenses or fang extensions. (*Really? That was a real thing? Why would anyone do that?*) Failure to disclose felony convictions or past indiscretions resulted in automatic disqualification.

Before dozing off, Mischa had gotten some clarification on that last one, because *indiscretions* was a *really* broad field. And she'd had some doozies, not even counting her recent panty-less walk of shame.

But, fortunately, none of Mischa's indiscretions made the list of concerns Barbie had. Apparently in the vampire world, *indiscretions* usually meant killing humans when in the throes of bloodlust.

Oopsie...don't you just hate it when that happens?

Miss Texas had jabbed her pointy little elbow into Mischa's ribs when she'd apparently started snoring. She'd startled awake with a muttered, "What the fuck?", only to find everyone in the room, Barbie included, giving her the stink eye.

She'd mumbled an apology, but no one seemed to be in a forgiving mood.

Try thirty or forty orgasms, ladies. Perks the mood right up.

But at that point, it didn't really matter because orientation was over. So, she'd collected her welcome bag and orientation booklet (which she could've just read on her own, thank you very much. The whole orientation process was really just a thinly veiled opportunity to let the contestants psych each other out) and strolled to the auditorium, where a photographer was going to be taking headshots of each contestant for the pageant's marketing efforts.

When she got there, she was surprised that Harper was missing. Mischa assumed her doctor's appointment was running late. But that presented somewhat of a challenge. She was pretty sure she was the only vampire in the room not wearing makeup, and something told her that Barbie would be pissed to have a headshot of a contestant sporting the *natural* look. Especially a headshot of *her*, since she was already on the pageant princess's shit list.

And that's when she saw something that would've stopped her heart if it still beat. Two somethings, actually. Somethings that most assuredly meant her day was about to get more…complicated.

First of all, the source of her walk of shame rock-bottom had just walked in, wearing a flannel work shirt, left unbuttoned over an ab-hugging, beat-up gray T-shirt. He was carrying some kind of complicated, heavy-looking lighting rig over one shoulder and a video camera and tripod over the other. A tool belt was slung around his lean hips and looked like it belonged there.

He was every girl's blue-collar fantasy made real, a walking Diet Coke commercial. And his focus was entirely on her. She could feel his gaze moving over her from the top of her head, to the pointy toes of the ridiculously complicated high-heeled shoes she'd borrowed from Harper.

Her nipples immediately went on high alert.

Christ, the no-fraternization with event staff policy suddenly had brand-new meaning for her. Apparently, she'd *fraternized* the hell out of the new lighting guy a few hours ago.

And he was currently eye-*fraternizing* her to the point that she was ready to jump him right there in front of an entire auditorium full of pageant contestants and assistants, policies be damned.

Next to him was another *something* that could prove to be problematic.

She was about five feet tall, not including her teased cloud of blond curls, and wore a smart vintage tweed suit and matching pillbox hat. She looked like she'd just stepped off the set of *His Girl Friday*. Not a modern remake, mind you, but the version from 1940.

Mischa had known many, many people (and creatures) in her life. She'd seen every bit of good, bad, and evil this city had ever known. Not much intimidated her anymore.

But this woman? This was the scariest bad-ass MOFO Mischa had ever met. She'd seen this woman reduce ancient vampires to tears. She'd seen this woman wrangle confessions to heinous crimes and dastardly plots out of every known species of supernatural creature. This woman had been known to make feral werewolves piss themselves in fear, and she never had to raise a fist or a weapon to do it.

Her mere presence meant Harper was desperate. She never called in this particular asset unless she had nowhere else to turn.

This woman was…gulp…Harper's mother.

Chapter Fourteen

Tina Petrocelli was the most naturally gifted empath Hunter had ever known. Looking her in the eye was like having someone tear open your brain and take a good long look inside. In all his years, he'd never met a human empath who was able to breach his mental shields, but Harper's mother did it with virtually no effort at all.

When he picked her up at Harper's request, he'd said nothing more than hello, and she'd frowned and asked him if he was OK. When he said he was fine, she'd snorted and said, "Yeah, sure, and I'm a dead ringer for Angelina Jolie."

She'd fortunately left it at that, because if she'd asked another question, Hunter probably would've spilled his guts, admitting how twisted and fucked up he was over Mischa. And that would've gotten back to Harper, who would've told Mischa, and wouldn't that have just been the cherry atop the shit sundae he was currently living?

The source of his continuous vexation was currently wringing her hands, watching him approach with Tina, her expression somewhere between joy and terror.

She's happy to see you, his pathetic heart practically sang.

His brain shut down that train of thought before it could go any further. *Of course she's happy to see you, you loser. She hadn't had sex or real blood in months, and you gave her both. You're a one-stop shop, all wrapped up in one handy, available, pathetically loyal package.*

He stopped so close to her that she had to crane her neck to look him in the eye. "Nice dress," he said.

It was most likely his body that had put voice to that particular sentiment, since it was his body—not his head or heart—that most appreciated the clingy black slip of nothing that hugged her delicate curves like, well, he had the night before.

The dress that made it pretty damn obvious she was cold. Or turned on.

Mischa blinked up at him, looking a little dazed. "Thanks," she said after swallowing hard. "It's Harper's."

"Jesus, Mary, and Joseph," Tina muttered, wrinkling her nose and waving her hands in the air between them as if she smelled something bad. "The lust and angst and need in the air between you two is choking me. Can you rein that in or something?"

If only.

Mischa cleared her throat and closed her eyes for a moment. When she opened them, she said, "Mrs. Petrocelli, it's nice to see you, but where's Harper? Is everything all right?"

She adjusted her hat daintily. "Oh, honey, she's mad enough to chew nails and spit tacks. Her doctor said her blood pressure was up and she's in danger of preeclampsia, so he put her on bedrest until the end of the pregnancy."

Mischa's eyes got wide. "Holy shit. Harper stuck in bed all day?"

Hunter was pretty much a man without fear, and that particular thought made even him a little nervous. Harper was a whirling dervish. Staying in bed all day would be torture for her. And for everyone around her, most likely.

"How's Riddick taking this?" Mischa asked.

"About as well as can be expected," Tina said. "I'm pretty sure he's not allowed back at the doctor's office, though, given how he yelled at everyone for letting this happen to his wife. Made some fairly creative death threats, too." She chuckled. "It was *so* cute."

Death threats from Noah Riddick could only be called *cute* by Tina Petrocelli. Those on the receiving end had been known to shit their pants.

Tina clapped her hands together. "So, long-story-short, I'm here to help you with your hair and makeup." In a stage whisper, she added, "And I'll see if I can pick up any negative feelings towards the missing girls while I'm at it, and Hunter here will take Riddick's place on the lighting crew."

Hunter didn't have to use his telepathic ability to realize the thought of Tina doing her hair pretty much scared Mischa shitless. He smirked at her, imagining her hair arranged in Tina's poufy, teased-to-within-an-inch-of-its-life style.

Mischa narrowed her eyes at him and, against his will, his smirk grew into a genuine smile. For some reason, irritating her had always been one of his favorite hobbies.

She held on to her irritation for a moment, but it faded slowly until she ended up smiling back at him—and damned if that smile didn't hit him on a visceral level.

"Oh, enough of that," Tina groused. "You're making me have hot flashes, for God's sake." She fanned herself with her hand before giving Hunter a shove. "You, go hang a light or something." Pointing a stern mom finger at Mischa, she added, "And you, show me to the dressing room so we can get you ready for your photo session."

He gave Tina a two-finger salute and a "yes, ma'am" before clicking his heels together old-school military style to set up the lighting rig.

Behind him, he heard Tina say, "He's cheeky. Cocky, too."

Mischa didn't say anything that he heard, but a second or two later, Tina gasped and said, "Oh, my God, I didn't mean it like that! Get your emotions out of the gutter, girl. I swear, before this is all over I'm going to end up turning a hose on the two of you."

And with that, Hunter did something he was pretty sure he hadn't done since before he'd been carted off the prison.

He laughed.

Chapter Fifteen

The next day just after dark, Mischa and Hunter sat in Harper and Riddick's bedroom, recounting the evening's events for Harper.

Propped up on about twenty pillows while Riddick rubbed her swollen feet, Harper looked like a queen—albeit an uncomfortable and agitated queen—addressing her court.

Given the sheer volume of food-laden trays surrounding the bed, Mischa assumed Riddick had moved the entire contents of the fridge so that everything was within his wife's reach.

"Where the hell is Benny with my damn cheesy tots?" she grumbled.

"I sent him away," Riddick said calmly, even as Harper's expression promised hellfire and brimstone. "We're watching your salt intake, remember? Too much salt raises your blood pressure, which isn't good for the baby."

Harper threw her head back against her pillows and groaned. "But I love salt! Salt is everything that is good and beautiful on this earth."

"You told me yesterday that doughnuts are everything that is good and beautiful on this earth," Mischa reminded her.

Her eyes lit up. "Ooohhh, doughnuts." She gave Riddick big, pleading eyes. "Can I have doughnuts?"

He sighed. "The doctor didn't say anything about fat and sugar, just salt."

Mischa called Benny and changed his cheesy tots mission to a doughnuts mission, which he accepted with minimal grousing. "He'll be here in twenty-five minutes," she said after disconnecting the call.

Mollified, Harper leaned back and rested her hands on her belly.

"So, did you get to talk to many of the other contestants?"

Mischa nodded. "Most of them were out of state with rock-solid alibis when the missing girls disappeared. Benny's done the research and cleared everyone except Miss Texas, Jaslene Sanchez, and Miss Utah, Emily Brooks. Emily seems nice enough. Quiet, a little shy. Your mom says her emotions are all pure, innocent joy to be there. She's probably not our girl. Texas is hard to read."

And she has really pointy elbows, Mischa thought, rubbing her ribs.

Harper frowned. "Hard to read how? Like she's a little guarded, or like she's a sociopath?"

"She's not a sociopath," Hunter said. "She has some emotions, but she only lets you see what she wants you to see. Her mental shields are impressive. If she doesn't want you to know what she's thinking or feeling, you won't."

Mischa felt jealousy grab her by the throat. "When did you talk to Miss Texas?"

He met her gaze steadily. "When she offered to blow me as soon as the competition was over."

Her jaw dropped. "Are you fucking kidding me? What a whore!" Then a treacherous thought crept into her mind. "What did you say?"

He smirked at her. "Would it matter to you?"

Yes! I love you, you fucking moron! Isn't it as obvious as the nose on your absurdly handsome face? The nose I kind of want to punch right now? And also, because you're mine, damn it!

But she didn't have the right to blurt any of that out. No matter how she felt, she had no real claim on him. She still needed to apologize for her behavior after he'd turned her. And, if she was being totally honest with herself, she should probably apologize for neck-raping him, too. But having that kind of talk in front of Harper and Riddick didn't seem prudent.

So, instead of blurting out the first thing that popped into her head, she blurted out the *second* thing that popped into her head, which probably wasn't much better. "Did you get to *talk* to any of the other contestants?"

"Kansas, Delaware, Hawaii, and one of the Dakotas." He shrugged. "Can't remember which one."

"All the big square states in the middle are the same as far as I'm concerned," Harper said, waving a hand dismissively. "I can never remember which one is which."

Mischa made a mental note to ensure that Kansas, Delaware, Hawaii and both Dakotas were miserable for the remainder of the competition. The innocent of the two Dakotas would just have to be considered collateral damage.

"What about the crew?" Riddick asked.

Hunter scowled. "All human and all there to scope out pretty girls who might be willing to turn them into vampires." He stabbed a finger at Mischa. "Stay away from that photographer, Vincent."

Harper leaned forward. "Why? Is he suspect?"

"No. I don't think he knows anything about the missing girls. I'm betting he's too busy trying to think of ways to get the remaining contestants into bed with him to even realize there *are* missing girls."

His glance back at Mischa was telling. Ha! She barely resisted the urge to throw her fist in the air triumphantly. She'd *thought* Vincent had shown her a little more attention than he'd shown the other girls. Hunter must have seen something about her in the photographer's thoughts.

So, Mr. Calm, Cool, and Detached wasn't as immune to her as he pretended to be. "Would that matter to you?" she taunted, throwing his own words back at him. "Jealous?"

He leaned toward her, and her gaze fell immediately to his mouth, which was irritatingly, enticingly close to her own.

"I'm over five hundred years old," he said through obviously clenched teeth. "I don't get *jealous*."

If she stuck her tongue out the slightest bit, she'd be able to run it over his bottom lip. "So why tell me to stay away from him?"

He raised a single brow, which was sexy and annoying all at the same time. "Can't have you disqualified before the competition even begins, now can we?"

He probably didn't even think about it because it was all old hat to him by now, but she was just starting to realize that she could pinpoint the smells related to certain emotions.

Oh, it was true. Every emotion had a distinct odor. Fear had a weak, urine-like smell to it. Anger smelled sharp and burned the nostrils a bit, almost like inhaling a fistful of pepper. Lust smelled sweet, like roasted marshmallows. Jealousy was faintly sour, like milk a few days past its expiration date.

And right now? Roasted marshmallows and sour milk. He was jealous. And he still wanted her.

Her heart did a little happy dance.

"Hey, Hunter," Harper said, "What would you do if Vincent laid so much as a finger on Mischa?"

"I'd rip his lungs out through his nose, turn them inside out, then cram them back down his throat," he said on a growl, not breaking eye contact with Mischa.

There was momentary silence in the wake of that pronouncement before everyone turned their attention back to Harper, who looked pretty damned pleased with herself.

Riddick cleared his throat, giving her a stern look. She shrugged, examining her nails. "What? I was getting bored. They were taking forever to get to the part where they both admitted they still want each other. I don't have all damn day, here."

"Actually, you do," he told her, gesturing to her belly and the bed around them.

She rolled her eyes, but grinned up at him. "Nuance. So, anyhoo, you two crazy kids get the hell out of here and work out your differences. I won't have the case compromised because you're going at it like cats and dogs."

"Sorry," Mischa mumbled at the same time Hunter mumbled, "It won't happen again."

"Damn straight it won't," Harper said, then moaned obscenely when Riddick dug his thumbs into the arch of her foot. He didn't look up from his task, but grinned and shook his head.

Mischa looked back at Hunter. "Clary's?"

Clary's was a pub a couple of blocks away from Harper and Riddick's apartment. It was mostly dark and quiet (except for karaoke night) and would serve quite nicely as neutral territory.

Hunter's nod was terse, but she'd take it as a victory. At least he wasn't running away from her anymore.

Chapter Sixteen

She was nervous.

If the hand-wringing and shifting eyes weren't a clear indication that Mischa was anything but comfortable sitting across from him, her scent made it obvious. Nervous energy had a faintly floral scent to it, and right now? It smelled like he was sitting in a whole fucking field of wildflowers.

He supposed he could understand it. He'd bailed on her—like a complete pussy—while she slept, leaving her to wonder what the hell was going on in his head.

He couldn't be of much help, there. It's not like he wasn't a fucking basket case, doing and saying shit that made absolutely no sense.

He just hadn't trusted himself to wake up with her. Hadn't trusted that he wouldn't end up begging her to stay and scaring her off again.

Her knee started bouncing under the table. He sighed. "There's no reason to be so nervous," he said, trying to project a calm energy he wasn't really feeling. "It's just you and me here."

She snorted. "Yeah, sure. Just me and the guy who hates me. Nothing to be *at all* nervous about."

Hunter frowned. "I don't hate you."

She either didn't hear him or didn't believe him, because she let loose with, "I've never really said I'm sorry for anything in my life, so I'm not very good at it, and the first time I need to do it—because I really, *really* need to do it—it's with someone who can't even stand to wake up with me in his bed. My instinct is just to run away, but Vi says I'll always be twisted if I keep running away, so I'm just—"

Hunter couldn't take it anymore. He leaned over the table and grabbed her hands. Her wide eyes flew to his and her mouth snapped shut. "Stop," he said quietly. "I don't hate you. I could never hate you."

If he was capable of hating her, he wouldn't be such a fucked-up mess right now.

Her lower lip trembled and he wanted nothing more than to kiss away any lingering nervousness she felt.

See? Fucked. Up. Mess.

"You don't owe me any apologies," he finally said.

She shook her head. "No, I really do. After you turned me, I was—"

He squeezed her hands. "Don't. I know. It was normal for you to be confused and scared. I had no right to expect anything different from you, and you had every right to hate me."

She was quiet for a moment, then, in a voice so raw with emotion that his own heart ached just hearing it, she whispered, "I didn't hate you. I couldn't. I lov—"

"No," he interrupted, his jaw so tight it actually hurt to force the word out. "Don't say that. Don't you dare tell me you love me right now."

Her smooth brow furrowed. "Why not?"

Because if you say it, I'll come across this table, kiss the hell out of you, and never let you go again? Because we'll fall back into the same old patterns—I chase, you run, I keep chasing, you keep running—time and time again for all eternity?

He cleared his throat. "Because I don't believe you."

She jerked back like he'd slapped her. "You think I'd lie about that?"

Christ, he'd really become a shit communicator since he was incarcerated. He scrubbed a hand over his face. "No. I think you're too confused right now to make a statement like that. You're…different now. What you may or may not have felt before…" he trailed off, shaking his head, "…isn't relevant right now. You have to figure out who you are and love yourself before you can love anyone else."

Her jaw visibly tightened, but she didn't look angry, just…resigned and a little sad. "You sound just like Vi. Did they have you watching *Dr. Phil* while you were in prison?"

He couldn't help but chuckle. "Hardly."

She gave him a sexy little smirk that was so familiar his heart ached. She might be different, but not *everything* had changed.

"So, what do we do now?" she asked, sounding hesitant. "I mean, it's not like we can avoid each other, not with both of us working for Harper. And frankly," she averted her eyes, the scent of flowers rising in the air between them again, "I don't want to avoid you. Can we start over? Can we be…friends?"

He let go of her hands and leaned back in his seat. Was it possible to be friends with a woman who'd ripped his heart out time and time again? One look at her hopeful, nervous face gave him his answer.

"I'd like that," he said quietly.

Her answering smile was the second most beautiful thing he'd ever seen in his unnaturally long life. The first, of course, being her face in the throes of an orgasm he'd just given her.

Don't go there, dumbass.

"There is one thing you have to let me apologize for, though."

He raised a brow at her when she hesitated.

She pointed to his neck. "The…um…neck raping. I got a little…out of control."

He snorted. Neck raping. As if there was anything nonconsensual about it. "You definitely don't have to apologize for *that*."

"So you didn't…mind?"

He met her gaze levelly. "I think I made it pretty clear I didn't *mind*."

If she was still human, she'd be blushing, if her scent was any indication. "Do you think the…attraction between us will be a problem?"

Yes. Every damn minute he was with her and not touching her. Or kissing her. Or inside her. "I can control myself if you can," he said, striving for a nonchalant, teasing tone. And failing miserably, he was pretty sure.

But true to form, her pointy little chin tilted defiantly and she shot back with, "I'm sure I can manage."

She offered him her hand as if to shake on their new arrangement. He made the mistake of accepting it and holding on too long. Her skin was so smooth, so soft…

Her gaze dropped to his lips and seemed to get stuck there for a moment.

Yeah, sure, he thought wryly. They could start over and just be friends.

And yet he'd agreed to try.

Seemed like Mischa wasn't the only one who was a little twisted.

Chapter Seventeen

The fitting for her bikini for the swimsuit competition was, without a doubt, the most humiliating experience of her life. And given some of her recent humiliations? Well, that was saying a whole fuckuva lot.

The wardrobe manager was a guy named Saul who was several inches shorter than her—and if his grizzled appearance was any indication—roughly seven hundred years old. And, no, he wasn't a vampire. He was just the oldest living human Mischa had ever seen in her life.

His advanced age didn't stop him from grabbing handfuls of her boobs while measuring her bust size, though. The horny old goat had tried to pawn it off as an accident, too. A side-boob brush she could write off, but a full-on grab and squeeze? Yeah, not so much. Saul was a pervert.

And in her capacity as an undercover investigator, she couldn't very well smack him around and risk drawing too much attention to herself.

Instead, she'd let her elbow "accidentally" swing back into his gut with enough force to double him over. She profusely—and sweetly—apologized, of course, but she was pretty sure he'd gotten the message not to fuck with her.

The one who hadn't gotten the message? Miss Texas.

Mischa wasn't sure if Jaslene was responsible for the disappearances of the former Miss New Jersey and Miss New York, but she was kind of starting to hope the bitch was guilty. At least then she'd be able to hate her with a good, just cause, instead of hating her because she looked at Hunter like she wanted to eat him for dinner.

When Mischa had reminded the woman—who was annoyingly beautiful with big blue eyes and shiny black hair that cascaded down her back in thick waves—of the rules prohibiting fraternization with event crew, she'd laughed a tinkling little laugh ripe with condescension.

"The show won't last forever," Jaslene had stage-whispered. "And after I win? He's mine."

Over my undead body, Mischa had thought.

It was then she decided that being friends with Hunter probably wasn't going to be easy. What if he decided to take Jaslene up on her offer—or if he eventually met someone else and fell in love? How was she supposed to sit idly by and watch the man she loved—and had carelessly tossed aside—ride off into the sunset with someone else?

Harper had advised her to bend him to her will. To take what she wanted through any means necessary. Her suggested means? Orgasms. Lots and lots of orgasms. She said orgasms made men more malleable. Typical Harper Hall advice.

Vi suggested a more straightforward, grown-up approach. Her plan for winning Hunter back involved them having an "open dialogue" about their feelings, and making when-you-did-that-I-felt-like-this statements to each other until they decided to either give their relationship another try, or abandoned it altogether.

But since she lacked Harper's confidence, and lacked the patience Vi's advice would require (and frankly Vi's advice sounded akin to Chinese water torture, anyway) her best hope at this point was to try her hand at being his friend and hope that he fell in love with her all over again. It was a possibility, right? Stranger things had happened. She hoped.

Benny elbowed her in the ribs, jarring her out of her musings. "Hand her that one. That's one I picked up. I'll bet that one gives her a vision."

Mischa handed Harper a gold key chain with Las Vegas spelled on the face in red glitter.

Benny and Mischa had spent the better part of the evening breaking into the apartments of the missing contestants and collecting various personal items. The hope was that one of the trinkets would trigger Harper's visions, giving them a clue about what had happened to the girls.

So far, they had *nada*.

Harper leaned back against her pile of pillows, shuffling the key chain from one hand to the other, eyes closed. After a moment, she dropped it on the bed next to her and wiped her palms on her sweatpants. "Ew," she said, nose wrinkling. "The former Miss New York had *quite* the time in Las Vegas. Let's just say that multiple dudes and one very confused-looking donkey were involved."

Mischa pantomimed gagging. "Sweet Christ, spare us the details."

Harper held up her hands, looking nauseated. "Hey, I'm not saying *anything* else. What happens in Vegas, stays in Vegas."

"Except herpes, man," Benny added helpfully. "That shit stays with you forever."

Harper studied him in expressionless silence for a moment before turning to Mischa. "Anyhoo, do you have anything else, or is that all of it?"

Mischa glanced back down at the now-empty box of knickknacks, jewelry, and clothing they'd stolen—or rather, *borrowed*—from the girls' apartments. "No, that's all we had. Should we go back and get more?"

Harper let out a frustrated sigh. "No. Honestly, I haven't had a helpful vision in a couple of months. I think the baby is messing with me, making me see only stuff I don't want to see. I think he/she has *quite* the sense of humor."

Like mother, like child, Mischa thought. Speaking of mothers... "Did your mom come up with any info?"

Harper snorted. "Other than gossip about how much you and Hunter want each other, and how Miss Michigan had butt implants? No, not so much."

So many questions, Mischa thought. Just how much did Hunter want her? Was it half as much as she wanted him? She hadn't even seen him during the last dress rehearsal, or after her final fittings. Where had he been all evening?

And beyond that...butt implants? Why would anyone want a *bigger* butt?

But Mischa kept her mouth shut, lest she come across as the pathetic, needy loser she felt like every time she was around Hunter.

"By the way," Harper said, "Did you work everything out with Hunter? Did he accept your apology?"

"He wouldn't let me apologize."

Benny let out a disgusted snort and shook his head. "Are we still talking about this? I already told you what you have to do to get him to forgive you. It's easy."

Harper frowned at him. "She can't just show him her boobs, Benny. The situation is much more complicated than that."

"There's no situation so complicated that boobs can't fix it," he said in a desert-dry, heart-attack serious tone.

Mischa wasn't about to admit that she *had* shown him her boobs and it hadn't made a difference. Maybe her boobs weren't as all-powerful as Benny seemed to think they were. "It doesn't really matter. We've decided to start over. To try just being friends."

Harper and Benny glanced at each other, then burst out laughing.

"What's so funny?" she asked, indignant.

Harper swiped at her watering eyes. "Oh, honey, it's hilarious that you think the two of you can just be friends."

Benny, still chuckling, added, "Yeah, sorry, but that's not gonna happen, hotness. There's too much history and zing there."

"Zing?" she asked, totally confused in a way that only conversations with Harper and Benny could confuse her.

Benny said, "You know how when you're in the same room with Harper and Riddick you kinda want to puke 'cause they're so damn cute together and so obviously banging each other every day?"

Mischa said, "Yes" at the same time Harper said, "Hey!"

"Well, that's zing, hotness. Chemistry. Disgusting, puke-inducing, sexy cuteness. And you've got it in spades with Hunter."

"So, you're saying you can't be friends with someone you have zing with?" Mischa asked.

His nod was immediate and emphatic. "Yep. That's what I'm saying."

Harper nodded in agreement. "Not with the kind of zing you have with Hunter, anyway."

Mischa threw her hands up in frustration. "Well, it's all I have right now, OK? I have to try." Because the alternative—letting him go entirely—was unthinkable.

Benny studied her for a moment before turning to Harper. "Ten bucks says they're back together—really together, none of this *just friends* shit—as soon as this competition's over."

"No way," Harper said. "They'll be together *before* the competition is over."

Benny rubbed his hands together gleefully. "Ooohhh, I'll take that bet, sister."

They did some kind of complicated hand shake to seal the bet while Mischa scowled at both of them. "Ten bucks says I start looking for new friends by the time the competition's over."

Harper laughed again. "If you haven't been doing that already, you're in worse shape than I thought."

Chapter Eighteen

Harper had made Hunter sit with her once years ago and watch a television show about people with bizarre psychological problems and addictions. On that show, he'd seen a woman who regularly sniffed gasoline, a man who was involved in a sexual relationship with his car, and a young girl who sucked on dirty diapers because she enjoyed the taste.

He'd watched each story with the same unblinking, horrified fascination that he watched each competition within the Miss Eternity pageant. It was a shocking, gaudy, tasteless spectacle. He wanted to look away. But just like that fascinatingly awful television show, he was powerless not to watch.

He had no idea what human pageants entailed, but vampire pageants included a strength competition (seeing women deadlifting thousands of pounds worth of free weights in evening gowns and heels wasn't something he would soon forget) and a vampire history trivia competition.

But his favorite? That was pretty easy. Without a doubt, Hunter's favorite competition so far was human-tossing for distance. The human was a volunteer, a thirty-four-year-old, two-hundred-ten-pound trucker from Rhode Island named Stan. He was a submissive, apparently, and visibly (ahem) *really* enjoyed being tossed.

Mischa's performance so far had surprised the hell out of him. After a shaky start with the choreographed opening dance number (she obviously wasn't accustomed to wearing heels), she quickly earned the judges' favor by placing second in the strength competition (someone should check Miss Texas for steroid use, in

Hunter's option), cleaned up in the trivia competition with a first-place win, and managed to toss Stan a foot further than any of the other competitors (He'd made some comment to her beforehand that she didn't care for, apparently, which had fueled her toss. He planned to have a chat with Stan about it later, and he could guarantee the bastard wouldn't enjoy it, submissive or not).

But through it all, she'd kept her head held high, showing a kind of self-confidence and poise she'd sometimes lacked as a human. She was an absolutely exquisite vampire, and everyone in the competition was now aware of it.

Which could make her a target if anyone had really done something to hurt the former Miss New York and Miss New Jersey.

But that and pretty much every other thought he'd ever had fled when Mischa walked out on stage in her swimsuit.

Although, *swimsuit* was a fairly generous term, in Hunter's opinion.

The whole thing seemed to be made of three eye patches and a few yards of ribbon. The deep emerald color was stunning against her golden skin, and Tina had woven matching green ribbons through her hair, which trailed down her back in soft waves. The high cut of the bottom of the suit and her five-inch heels gave her the appearance of being much taller than she actually was, and emphasized the sleek, toned muscles of her calves and thighs.

The small audience erupted in wild applause and whistles, and even from his perch on the lighting catwalk above the stage, he could see her features tighten in discomfort. She was embarrassed.

It was the first time since the beginning of the competition that she'd looked anything other than completely at ease in her own skin. His chest tightened in sympathy.

Hold your head high, love. You're the most beautiful woman in the room. In the world. You have no equal.

Her face registered a flicker of surprise before her gaze shot unerringly to his, letting him know she'd received his mental message. He smiled at her.

Her answering smile was a danger to his peace of mind. Too beautiful. Too bright.

And that's when the red laser dot appeared on her chest, right over her heart.

No, please, not again.

***

One minute, she was walking across the stage in her pitiful excuse for a bikini, praying to the God of double-sided tape that her boobs didn't pop right out of the top, smiling up at Hunter as he paid her the single best compliment ever uttered (well, *thought in her direction*, technically) and the next, she was rolling on the floor with him on top of her.

The sounds of shattering glass and shrill screams sounded all around them. People were knocked from their chairs as the humans in the audience stampeded to the exits. Her fellow contestants dove into the empty orchestra pit and cowered together, crying.

And all the while, Mischa wondered what the hell was going on.

Her eyes flew to Hunter's face, which was right next to hers as he shielded her with his body, one hand cupping the back of her head protectively.

She gasped as she noticed a red stain creeping across his chest, saturating his white T-shirt. "Someone tried to kill you!" she blurted.

The look he swept her way was a blend of concern, anger, and pity. It was the pity that really made her rethink the situation.

He'd been on the catwalk high above the stage. They were now on the floor, with him on top of her. If someone had been aiming for him, she wouldn't have needed rescuing.

"They weren't after me," he confirmed. "They were after you."

She swallowed hard. "Well…shit."

Chapter Nineteen

Mischa paced from one side of Harper's bedroom to the other, gnawing on her thumbnail as Riddick dug the bullet out of Hunter's back.

"Well, I think we can safely assume the missing girls didn't just get shy about their swimsuits and drop out of the competition," Harper said, digging enthusiastically into the cherry cheesecake resting on her lap.

Hunter took a deep swallow of the whiskey Riddick had pressed into his hand. "I'd say that's likely," he said dryly.

"I still don't know why you brought him here, Mischa," Riddick grumbled, digging into Hunter's back with a pair of tweezers. "I don't need crazy gun-toting vampire killers coming after you *at my house*, where my *pregnant* wife is on bedrest."

Rushing Hunter here hadn't been her finest moment, of that she was certain. Hunter couldn't reach the bullet hole to dig the bullet out himself, she certainly couldn't do it (she'd rather dig into her own flesh than his), and he'd refused to be taken to a hospital.

It had taken her a moment to realize he probably hated hospitals because the last time he'd been in one, she'd died and he'd been carted off to prison after bringing her back as a vampire. Not too many good memories there, she'd imagine.

But the bullet couldn't stay in his back, and without a better option, she'd panicked and brought him to Harper and Riddick. She hadn't even stopped to change out of her bikini. Thank God Harper had given her a T-shirt and pair of sweats to throw over the damn thing. And still, even though she agreed with him, Riddick's comment irked the bejesus out of her.

"Your concern for our welfare is heart-warming, Riddick," she said, adopting the same dry tone Hunter had used with Harper.

"Of course I'm concerned," he said, not taking his eyes off his task. "If the two of you died, Harper would be devastated, and she doesn't need that kind of stress right now. I just don't want your shit ending up at my door."

Mischa looked to Harper for some kind of intervention— Riddick had just said that his only concern for her welfare was the potential impact it might have on his wife, for Christ's sake—and found no help there. Harper was snout-down in her cheesecake, cradling it like a newborn, looking beyond content.

Mischa hissed in sympathy as Riddick finally, *finally* pulled the bullet out of Hunter's back.

He held it up for her inspection. "Wooden. If it had hit an inch to the left, he'd be dust right now."

"Christ, Riddick," Harper said around a mouthful of cherries and cream cheese, "don't sugar-coat it. Tell it like it is."

His brow furrowed. "Well, what do you want me to do, lie? Hug him and tell him everything will be OK?"

She smirked. "That'd be super-helpful. Would you?"

He shuddered. "Fuck no."

"I'm just saying you could be a little more sensitive, babe," she told him.

He looked revolted by the idea, but muttered, "Sorry," to Mischa and Hunter as he put the bullet in a plastic bag.

Mischa sat down on the end of the bed next to Hunter and put her hand on his knee, completely powerless to *not* touch him. He'd almost died. For her.

The thought alone made her throat close up. She couldn't imagine a world without him in it.

"Did you get a look at the shooter?" Harper asked.

Mischa shook her head. "No. When you're on stage, the lights are right in your face. You can't see anything but shadows and movement in the audience, no faces."

Hunter rolled his shoulder and Mischa winced when he did. God, that had to hurt. "I didn't see anyone, either," he said. "I only saw the light from the rifle's scope on her chest."

He laid his hand on hers. Apparently he was having trouble *not* touching her as well.

"My mom called and said the police showed up about ten minutes ago. She'd already talked to all of the contestants and feels like they're not directly involved," Harper said. "She wants to take another run at Miss Utah, though. Said she was looking a little squirrelly."

Mischa nodded. "It doesn't seem like anyone is nervous or hiding anything, or holding any grudges. Miss Texas is the only one there who could even be considered…edgy at all."

"What about the crew?" Riddick asked. "Building maintenance?"

"They're clean," Hunter answered. "Nothing unusual at all. No malice towards any of the contestants. No signs of guilt."

Harper tapped her spoon against her lower lip thoughtfully. "So, none of our powers are working on this one. We're going to have to solve this thing *Cagney and Lacey* style."

Mischa blinked at her. "With bad haircuts and ill-fitting jackets with shoulder pads?"

Harper scowled. "No, smartass. Detective work. Actual detective work."

It would probably take an actual detective to figure out why Harper referenced that particular show when there were literally hundreds of less obscure, more current options, but Mischa thought better of pointing that out. Harper was probably onto something. "I could go back to the auditorium. Talk to the police. See what they've been able to find."

Hunter's fingers tightened around hers. "I'll go. I don't want you anywhere near that place tonight."

Harper took another bite of cheesecake before mumbling, "That auditorium is probably the safest place she could be right now. It's crawling with cops, according to my mom. And they're looking for the two of you, anyway. You're the only witnesses they haven't been able to locate for questioning."

Riddick handed Mischa the plastic bag with the bullet in it. "Take them this. I'm sure they'll completely fuck up the investigation, but it probably belongs in evidence."

Riddick's eagerness to get rid of them must have rankled Hunter, too, if his scowl was any indication.

Mischa shook her head, turned her palm up, and laced her fingers with his. "Back to the scene of the crime?" she asked.

He couldn't look any less enthused as he said, "Sure. Why not? An evening with the police should top the evening off nicely."

Chapter Twenty

The Vampire Crimes Unit (or, VCU for short) was pretty much a joke. If it hadn't been mandated by law, the Whispering Hope Police Department most likely wouldn't have established a "spook crimes" division (as the other divisions not-so-lovingly referred to it). So, the detectives assigned to investigate vampire crimes were either the department's weakest and laziest detectives, or the detectives with...behavioral issues. The ones who didn't play well with others.

Detective Lucas Cooper fell into the latter category.

A wolf shifter who'd long ago given up the pack life, Lucas was a loner who had little use the rest of his department or, well, anyone really. He was a good cop, charming when he needed to be, but otherwise a grumpy curmudgeon.

As a fellow grumpy curmudgeon, Mischa had always liked Lucas. But right now? Not so much.

He'd dragged them to the police station as soon as they showed up at the auditorium, and now, she sat next to Hunter in an interrogation room, answering the same questions over and over again.

She rubbed her temples, feeling completely drained. "Lucas, I told you already, the pageant rep thinks two contestants were forced into dropping out, and the police—*you*—wouldn't investigate. So, she hired Harper, who sent me in to talk to the other contestants and see what I could dig up. I have no idea who shot at me."

Lucas had his cop face on. When he wasn't purposefully erasing all emotion from his face like that, he was a seriously good-looking guy. Square jaw, chiseled cheek bones, messy dark blond hair...he was undeniably hot. But with the cop face on? Mischa just found him...annoying.

He turned his gaze to Hunter. "You don't work for Harper. Why were you there?"

"I took Riddick's place," Hunter said, arms crossed over his chest, doing his own version of the impassive, annoying cop face.

Lucas mimicked his posture. "And why did you need to take Riddick's place? What's he doing that's more important than taking care of this case?"

Mischa didn't like the implication that Riddick was blowing off the case. "He's at home with his pregnant wife, who was just put on bedrest, OK?" she snapped. "None of this is relevant. And why do you sound so suspicious? You know we're not suspects."

His cop face remained intact, but he flinched at the mention of Harper. "Is she OK?"

Not that he really ever talked about his feelings, but it was fairly obvious that Lucas had been in love with Harper at some point. Maybe still was. But from the moment Riddick entered the picture, Harper was all his. No competition.

To say she was sympathetic to his plight—loving someone you couldn't be with—was a gross understatement.

"She's fine. Angry that she can't be more involved in the case, but otherwise fine," Mischa said gently.

He was quiet for a moment, eyes lowered and masking his expression, as he digested that bit of information. Then, when his lashes lifted again, he was back in full-on cop mode. "It's nothing personal, Mischa. Everyone is treated as a suspect until proven otherwise."

She frowned at him. "I thought everyone was innocent until proven guilty."

"Not in the VCU."

Well that was just...sad. She sighed. "Have we answered enough of your questions to be cleared of suspicion for now? At least until someone finds the missing girls tied up in our basement or something, right?"

Note to self: cops are miserable, humorless fucks. Mischa would just file that little tidbit away for future use.

"I couldn't give a shit about the missing girls right now," Lucas grated out through clenched teeth. "We don't have any evidence to suggest anything bad happened to either of them. I care about finding whoever opened fire in the auditorium. So, until I'm able to do that, your case is shut down and you're out of the competition."

Mischa's jaw dropped. "You can't do that!"

"I can, and I will. It's not safe for you to be in there, anyway. Someone obviously doesn't like you. My guess is someone is trying to clear a path so that his or her favorite can win, and you're in the way. And since you haven't really figured jack out yet on your own yet, I'm gonna need you to stay out of *my* way while I figure this all out."

Her eyes narrowed on him. "You can't kick me out now. Now more than ever you need someone on the inside! And having the cops crawling all over the competition—all big and obvious—might send the shooter underground altogether. You. Need. Me."

He leaned forward. "I don't need anyone. And I won't use you as bait to draw this guy out. I'm doing you a favor by forcing you out."

Oh, of all the arrogant, testosterone-stunted logic she'd ever heard in all her life...well, she'd just see about that. Mischa pulled out her cell phone and dialed the one person she knew could tip the odds in her favor with Lucas.

Lucas raised a brow at her. "I'm not charging you with anything, Mischa. You don't need to lawyer up."

She snorted. He *wished* she was lawyering up. Her call was answered on the first ring. "Riddick, put Harper on the phone," she growled.

Hunter relaxed beside her, smirking at the now-nervous-looking cop.

"Harper," she said when her friend answered. "Lucas says we're off the case and I'm out of the competition."

"Mischa, hang up the phone," Lucas hissed. "There's no reason to drag her into this. I've made myself clear. You're absolutely not going back undercover. That's an order."

She had to hold the phone away from her ear as Harper shouted an expletive and made an anatomically improbable suggestion for what Lucas could do with his *order*.

When Harper was done, Mischa smiled sweetly and handed the phone to Lucas. "She'd like to speak with you."

He shook his head as he took the phone, giving her a look that could peel paint. "You don't fight fair."

She shrugged, completely unrepentant.

"Harper," he said, somewhat uncertainly. "How are you doing, doll-face?"

He listened for a moment and began tugging at his eyebrow nervously. "Yeah, I know you are. But I'm trying—"

More listening, followed by, "No, *of course* I'm not trying to take food out of your baby's mouth. I just—"

What followed was a ten-minute pattern of Lucas listening, attempting to address whatever Harper was saying, being interrupted, then listening some more. His expression went from nervous, to angry, to irritated, and back to nervous again several times before he finally rested his forehead in his palm and muttered, "Jesus. Fine. You win. No, I said *fine*."

And with that, he disconnected the call and slid the phone across the table back to Mischa. "So?" she asked.

He rolled his head around on his shoulders a few times before sighing, and saying (in the most world-weary voice Mischa had ever heard), "You have 48 hours. Wrap up your case by the close of the competition, one way or the other. Then I take over."

She smiled and started to thank him, but he interrupted her with, "Don't even fucking say it. If anyone was paying a damn bit of attention to what we do in this unit, I wouldn't be able to do a fucking thing to help you. And trust me when I say I'd rather not be helping you, Mischa. So don't you fucking dare *thank* me."

And with that, he shoved them both out the door, slamming it shut behind them.

Feeling pretty pleased with herself, she smiled up at Hunter. "So, feeling like helping me solve this thing?"

He chuckled. "I'm assuming that if I say no you'll sic Harper on me?"

She raised a brow at him. "If Harper hadn't gotten the job done, I was calling Tina."

He shuddered, then shook his head, smiling. "Remind me never to piss you off." Offering her his arm, he added, "Shall we, *friend?*"

Mischa took his arm and ignored the sour feeling in her gut she experienced at the word *friend*. Sucking up her feelings and ignoring her instinct to tell him that he was, in no uncertain terms, *hers* in a very not-just-friends kind of way, she gave him a cheery, "We shall."

Chapter Twenty-one

By the time they got back to the convention hall, the police and a majority of the contestants had left. The janitorial staff was hard at work, fixing the damage the gunman and horde of stampeding humans had left in their wake.

Hunter was immediately asked to help with the cleanup, and agreed (somewhat reluctantly, and only after a lengthy debate) to let her snoop around backstage on her own.

Mischa walked past a janitor on her way to the backstage area and nearly blacked out as the smell of ammonia, dirty mop water, and—oddly enough—flowers assailed her nostrils. She shook her head. Why on earth did cleaners try to hide unpleasant odors with floral scents?

She found Tina patting a sobbing Miss Utah's shoulder soothingly, handing her tissues. The poor sobbing girl didn't notice that the seemingly endless supply of tissues was coming from Tina's bra. Mischa shuddered.

"Are you all right, dear?" Tina asked as she approached, concern clear in her expression, even as her voice remained completely calm.

"I'm fine," she murmured. She gestured to Emily, who honked despondently into her tissue. "What's going on here?"

Emily let out a keening cry that made Mischa cringe. "This is all my fault!" she wailed.

Mischa turned her attention back to Tina as Emily continued to sob. She raised her hands in the universal what-the-hell gesture.

Tina handed Emily another bra tissue and said quietly, "A few years ago, when she was still human, Emily had a stalker. He quit bothering her when she was in a car crash and someone on the scene changed her into a vampire. She assumed it was all over. Until today."

Mischa knelt down so that she was eye-level with Emily. "What did your stalker do to you, Emily?"

She sniffled, her big green eyes looking confused. "To me? Oh, he didn't do anything to me."

Mischa was beyond tired. She'd had to prance around in a too-small swimsuit in front of a studio audience. She'd had to argue with—and threaten—the cops to keep her case moving. She'd watched Riddick dig a bullet out of Hunter's back—a bullet that had been meant for her. She really, *really* lacked the patience necessary to deal with this sobbing, emotional wreck of a vampire.

Tina picked up on her impatience (and, if she was being totally honest, her desire to throttle poor, hysterical Emily) and said, "Her stalker sent her notes and flowers. Let her know he was watching and was ready to *help* her," she made finger quotes on *help*, "get everything she wanted in life."

Emily sniffled again. "In the beginning, it was really kind of sweet, you know? It was kind of nice knowing that someone…loved me and wanted to watch over me."

Sure, 'cause nothing said "sweet" like a stranger watching you from afar. Mischa barely refrained from rolling her eyes. "I'm guessing his idea of 'helping' wasn't real helpful?"

"No, it totally was," she said, lip trembling. Mischa braced herself for another wail, but Emily pulled herself together, adding, "Just not for anyone but me."

Tina patted her shoulder again. "When Emily was graduating high school, she missed being valedictorian by a smidge, maybe a fraction of a grade point."

"Fucking home-ec," Emily muttered.

Mischa pinched the bridge of her nose, silently reaching deep for any trace of patience she might have left.

"On graduation day," Tina went on, "the valedictorian had an...accident. She broke her leg and Emily got to deliver her speech after all."

The look on Tina's face made it clear that the Valedictorian's *accident* hadn't been quite as accidental as it could've been. "The stalker pushed her?"

Emily nodded. "He sent me a note with some flowers saying how great my speech had been, and that he was glad he'd 'taken care of' everything to make sure I got to deliver it."

"Did you go to the police?" Mischa asked.

Emily didn't look her in the eye as she twirled her long red curls around her finger and said, "No. I was kind of...glad he'd done it. Jessica was a horrible girl! She'd been picking on me since elementary school. Made everyone call me 'Giraffe.' It was humiliating!"

Mischa had been called "Midget" in elementary school, so "Giraffe" didn't seem too bad, in her opinion. And Emily did have really long, skinny legs and a long, slender neck, which gave her a distinctly giraffe-like appearance...

Mischa gave herself a sharp mental slap to get back on track. "What happened after that, Emily?"

"I started getting into pageants after that."

Emily went on to tell stories of girls who'd been performing better than her in various pageants, only to mysteriously end up skipping town in the middle of the night, or to get disqualified when events from their pasts that no one could possible know came to light. Emily eventually won every pageant she ever entered, which brought them full circle.

The urge to throttle the girl grew. "And you never told the police?" Mischa practically shouted.

Emily cringed away from the anger in her tone. "No one died! He was just giving me an advantage." Her chin came up a bit. "I never had an advantage before."

Foster care, Mischa knew immediately. In the barrio where she'd grown up, foster care kids all had the same hurt, deep and dark, in their eyes. Emily had the look of a former foster care kid.

Mischa felt her first twinge of sympathy for Emily. Hadn't she, after all, taken the "advantage" Sentry had offered her? And she'd walked away from her family without a second thought. Could she honestly say that she wouldn't have kept a secret admirer (or, avenger, as the case may be) to herself?

Emily dabbed at her melting mascara. "It all stopped after my car accident, anyway. Once I was a vampire, I guess my stalker decided I didn't need any other advantages." She looked contrite as she muttered, "Until now."

"And you didn't say anything to the cops tonight, either?"

Emily looked a little defensive this time. "I was scared, OK? I'm still not entirely sure why I told Tina. I just…had to."

Tina had the grace to look a little contrite. She must've felt that Emily was holding something back and used her powers to push her into confessing. Bless her intrusive heart.

"Emily, honey," Tina said, "the former Miss New York and Miss New Jersey…do you know what happened to them?"

She looked positively miserable. "No. I didn't really think anything of them dropping out—I mean, the guy hasn't contacted me since my accident—but then…I got these."

Emily gestured behind her, and in an expensive-looking glass bowl full of water, Mischa saw two fragrant white flowers floating lazily. They were huge and delicate looking, with dainty, spiky bases. She'd never seen anything like them.

"It's what he's always sent me," Emily whispered. "I looked it up one time. They're Kadupul flowers. Super rare. They only grow in some forest in Sri Lanka. They bloom at midnight and die at dawn."

Much like a vampire, Mischa thought, more creeped out by Emily's stalker than ever before. Had he planned her car accident? Did he always intend to make her a vampire so that he could be with his rare and beautiful flower forever?

Metaphor flowers. Now she'd seen it all.

"When did you get these?" Tina asked.

"They weren't here before the swimsuit competition. But when I came back to grab my stuff after the shooting, after I talked to the cops, they were here."

"Note?" Mischa asked.

Emily handed a tiny scrap of heavy, cream-colored card stock over to Mischa, who immediately gripped it by only the corners—*you never know, maybe the dude was dumb enough to leave prints*. Three words were printed on the card in some kind of elaborate, script-y font.

Soon, my love.

Great, Mischa thought. He was escalating. Her psych training at Sentry had taught her that stalkers weren't usually willing to stay in the background for long. They tended to step up their attentions when they felt the object of their fixation was slipping away from them. Maybe this guy felt that once Emily won Miss Eternity, she'd be beyond his reach unless he made a major move.

"Doesn't explain why he shot at me, though," Mischa murmured.

Tina shot her an incredulous look and snorted. "Duh. You were winning!"

Emily nodded emphatically when Mischa looked skeptical. "Oh, it's true. I sneaked a peek at the judges' scorecards while they were talking to the cops, and you were in the lead by several points." She sighed wistfully. "Your swimsuit was *awesome*. Saul obviously liked you the best."

If being his favorite meant getting groped and having to wear nothing but shoelaces and glitter onstage, she'd rather be at the bottom of his pervy little wish list.

Mischa turned to Tina. "You didn't mention any of this to Lucas, did you?"

She shook her head. "Harper told me not to for two days. Plus, I could tell he was just dying to pull you from the competition, so I thought keeping quiet for the moment was a better way to go."

Tina Petrocelli was a lot of things. Dumb wasn't one of them.

"I'm going to have Benny and Leon check on a few things. Will you stay with Emily for the rest of the night? In case this guy decides to make contact?"

She made a mental note to ask Lucas to put extra patrols on Tina's house. No telling what Harper would do if she found out Mischa had put her mom in harm's way.

"Sure thing." Tina grabbed Emily's hand. "My darling," she said with enthusiasm, "you are coming home with me tonight. I make a mean Bloody Juan. And my son, Michael—he's single and just started medical school if you can believe that—will just *love* you."

Emily looked confused, but seemed as enticed by the idea of pig's blood and tequila as she was by the idea of a single med student. "OK," she said with a shrug and a little smile.

Mischa watched them go, shaking her head.

Emily had no way of knowing it, but when faced with choosing between a creepy stalker and a night with Tina Petrocelli, most people would take their chances with the stalker.

Chapter Twenty-two

After stopping by his apartment to grab a change of clothes, Hunter drove Mischa back to her place. He told her it wasn't safe for her to be alone, in case Emily's stalker decided to take another shot at her. And that was the truth. But also...

He'd come too close to losing her—again—to not be with her now. Even if all he did was watch over her while she slept, it was necessary. He couldn't explain it.

Just another symptom of how far gone he was over this woman. Always had been.

He was starting to not see it as pathetic, though. It just...was.

Looking around, he decided that if he had only her apartment to go by, he'd guess that nothing had changed over the past year. Cool, neutral tones on the walls, books neatly lined up on the shelves by her fireplace—arranged alphabetically, of course. Sleek, modern furniture. Nothing frivolous or personal scattered about. Not a single throw pillow or knick-knack out of place.

It was the exact opposite of the chaotic Crayola explosion Harper lived in. Mischa's space was all about precision, function, and order.

His heart clenched at the thought of how painful it must be for her to have her neat, orderly life in such upheaval.

Hunter sighed and forced himself to sit on the couch.

Don't snoop around her apartment like a damn stalker, dumbass.

Mischa emerged from the bathroom in a cloud of steam, hair wet and tumbling over her shoulders in loose waves, legs peeking out from beneath a knee-length gray T-shirt. His, he recognized immediately. The one she must've worn home after their last night together.

He ignored the sudden tightening in his chest. He'd been a complete idiot to leave her, alone, in his bed.

Her eyes moved over his torso, reminding him he'd thrown his torn and bloody shirt away after his shower and hadn't bothered putting another one on yet.

"You look..." she swallowed hard, "...really good." She hastened to add, "The bullet wound is almost gone, I mean."

And you look like my every fantasy made real.

He wanted her so badly. To feel her soft skin against his. To hear her whisper his name as he slid into her. Deep, deep into her...

"Can we...talk?"

Talk? Was he still capable of that when she this close to him, half-naked? He wasn't sure, but he nodded.

She sat down next to him with her legs tucked up underneath her. When her eyes met his, he felt the usual invisible string that seemed to bind them together tighten, urging him to lean toward her. He caught himself before he could do something stupid. Like see how quickly he could get her clothes off and coax her into making the same throaty, breathless sounds she'd made the last time they made love.

He closed his eyes, calling himself a thousand kinds of fool. Weak. That's what he was. Weak.

She sighed. "I have so many problems, Hunter. I'm a complete mess."

Welcome to the club. "It's to be expected. The transition from human to vampire is difficult." Or so he'd heard. He was so damn old he couldn't remember his.

"It's not even all about the transition." She paused, looking embarrassed. "Vi says my instincts are all wrong. She convinced me that I need to do the opposite of what my instincts tell me to do so that I can reprogram myself to not be so...twisted anymore."

He frowned, not liking that word at all. "You're not twisted."

You're beautiful and strong and smart, and the only thing I ever really wanted in this world.

Her little self-deprecating smile made the tightening in his chest exponentially worse. "It's nice of you to say that, but Vi's right. I'm a runner."

Well, at least you're not Pepé Le Pew. "What's your instinct telling you to do now?"

"Run. Leave you alone. Do anything but try and apologize again…or tell you how I feel right now."

That sounded horrible. He opened his mouth to tell her so, but she cut him off with, "So, here it goes."

And with that, she straddled him, tightening her thighs around his hips, locking her fingers behind his neck.

His hands went automatically to her hips, fingers tightening, digging into smooth, soft flesh. This couldn't happen again, he thought. At least not until they'd had an actual conversation. Gotten a few things straight. But…

God, she was perfection in his arms. All warm, soft curves and sweet-smelling skin.

But sweet-smelling perfection aside, it was ultimately the vulnerability in her eyes that destroyed every argument he'd ever had for pushing her away. She never let anyone see this side of her, and it's what made him fall for her in the first place all those years ago.

She was different now, but…not. And he loved her as much now as he ever had. Maybe more.

His life had been hell over the past months, and if it didn't work out with them this time…he didn't really want to think about where he'd be.

So, he supposed it was time for that conversation they should've had months ago. "What are you—"

"I've asked pretty much everyone for advice on how to talk to you, how to make things right between us."

In the distant recesses of his brain it made him sad that she had to ask for advice about how to talk to him, but with her straddling him and only a few layers of cotton and denim between them, he wasn't sure his brain was in any condition to feel any particular way about…anything, really.

"And what did everyone tell you to do?" he asked, surprised he actually managed to sound so coherent.

She watched him through lowered lashes and licked her lips. "Well, Harper said I should bend you to my will. Force you to listen, then take what I want."

"So, loot and pillage, huh?" That seemed perfectly Harper-esque. "Not a terrible plan."

She laughed, which made her braless breasts jiggle, throwing off his concentration once again. "Unless the person you're trying to pillage is much, much stronger than you."

You might be surprised. He certainly wasn't feeling very strong at the moment.

"Benny's advice was the simplest."

How could it be anything but? "And what did Benny advise you to do?"

Mischa bit her lip, looking embarrassed. "Show you my boobs."

He barked out a surprised laugh and silently took back any uncharitable thoughts he'd ever had about Harper's little halfer friend. "I've always liked Benny."

She smiled, then lowered her lashes again. "Vi suggested we have a grown-up conversation. Maybe try a few of her psychology tricks."

Hunter had grown up in a time before psychology even existed. To say he was skeptical of its benefits was an understatement. But, it was Dr. Marchand's advice that had convinced Mischa to jump into his lap, so he supposed he shouldn't argue too much. "What kind of psychology tricks?"

"We take turns with 'I like it when' and 'I don't like it when' statements."

Seemed harmless enough. He shrugged. "Sure. Why not? Although, I don't think we should rule out Benny's advice all together."

She surprised him by whipping off her shirt and tossing it across the room. "His idea isn't entirely without merit," she said with a nervous chuckle, "and I'll take whatever advantage I can get."

He couldn't hold back his groan. Benny's plan was *genius*, because Mischa had perfect breasts, and Hunter found that he was absolutely powerless against them. He'd give her anything she wanted in that moment. His heart, his body, the world…whatever. It didn't matter. If she wanted it, it was hers.

He could almost span her entire ribcage with his hands. She arched into him as he skated his thumbs over her nipples, which immediately hardened. "And we're going to talk…like this?"

She just smiled at him.

He swallowed hard. "I'd say this…gives you a huge advantage."

She tipped her head to the side, studying him. "Well, Vi said I needed to stop running. I certainly can't run while I'm on your lap. Topless."

If he was still human, he'd be sweating right now, expending every bit of energy and strength he had to keep from tossing her over his shoulder and carrying her to bed. "OK, so who goes first?"

She glanced around. "We're supposed to have something to hold, first. Whoever is holding the…thing we choose…is the only one allowed to speak. Vi had some kind of 'talking stick' in her office, but I don't have anything like that. It could theoretically be anything, I guess. Anything that fits in your hand."

Hunter raised a brow at her questioningly and palmed her breast.

Her brows flat-lined. "Really?" she asked dryly. "I thought you were an ancient vampire, not a twelve-year-old boy."

He shrugged again. "If your breast is the talking stick, it'll make it even harder for you to run away."

Mischa frowned at him and he stared back at her, as guilelessly as he could manage. She eventually rolled her eyes and smacked his hand away. "Fine. But I'm going first."

She cupped her breast and said, "I don't like it when you…aren't with me."

He didn't waste any time replacing her hand with his own before murmuring, "I don't like it when you aren't with me, either."

She closed her eyes for a moment and laid her hand over his before he could pull it away. "You leave this one here," she whispered. "I have two. We'll just make the left one the talking stick from now on."

He would've laughed if he wasn't so damned turned on. And with that, she cupped her other breast and said, "I like it that…no matter how confused and twisted and fucked up I am, you're still here." She shook her head, tears glistening in her eyes. "I like it that…after all the horrible things I said to you after you turned me, you forgave me, and even took a bullet to protect me. Again. I like it that…you're the best man—vampire or human—that I've ever known."

There it was, he thought. That vulnerability again. She was speaking from her heart, something she almost never did. It was damned beautiful and damned humbling that she let him see this side of her.

Hunter held her gaze as he took her hand, turned it over slowly, and kissed the heart of her palm before laying it in her lap and taking the "talking stick" from her. He now cupped both breasts, and he damn near swallowed his tongue when she arched slightly, pushing her hardened nipples into his palms.

He cleared his throat and said, "I like it that you…are the strongest, smartest, most selfless woman I've ever known. I don't like it when you…doubt you're everything I've ever wanted in this world."

She blinked furiously, trying to blink away her tears, and laid both her hands over his on her breasts. "I don't like… knowing you could have anyone and not understanding why you chose me."

OK, psychology games are done. "You don't understand why I chose you?"

She shook her head and bit her lip before saying, "The...not understanding is what made me run after you turned me. I guess, even in the beginning, I always thought you'd eventually leave me."

His brow furrowed. "Why on earth would you think that?"

"Because I'm *me* and you're *you*," she said. "I've never been the girl that gets a guy like you. I was the smart girl in high school. The girl boy's cheated off of in math class, not the one they dated."

Now he was well and truly confused. "What do you mean a 'guy like you'? I never went to school a day in my life. They didn't even have schools in Lakota territory in 1492. If you knew how to hunt and fish and fight, you were good."

She sighed and lowered her head. "I'm messing this all up again. I'm just trying to say that I didn't understand then, but *now* I understand that no matter what I do, no matter how messed up I am or who else out there might be better for you, you'll always be here for me. For someone like me, that's huge." Her voice broke and she shook her head impatiently before adding, "So huge."

Someone like me. Someone who was accustomed to being alone, abandoned, and misunderstood, he knew immediately. God, she was breaking his heart.

"I was wrong to run from you," she added. "And if I had it all to do over again, I would do *everything* different. I would've never let you go."

He didn't have to look into her mind to see the truth in words. It was written all over her face, in those expressive, bottomless dark eyes. Want spiked through his body. Everything he'd ever needed was within reach. All he had to do was grab for it.

Hunter leaned forward and captured her mouth with his for a quick, hard kiss. "I think we've probably talked enough for a while, don't you?"

Her eyes fluttered shut. "Oh, thank God."

Chapter Twenty-three

The first time Hunter had kissed her all those years ago, she'd been so shocked and panicked she hadn't really been able to enjoy how he felt, how he tasted.

Now she could appreciate that he tasted like heat and strength and heaven and sex all wrapped up in one muscular-but-not-bulky, narrow-hipped, sinfully perfect package.

And it didn't matter that they'd kissed hundreds of times since that first time. It only took a mere whisper of his lips against hers to send a jolt of heat through her entire body. And *right* now? She felt like she had lava running through her veins instead of blood.

They made out and groped on the couch for what felt like hours, and she was more turned on than she'd ever been. It felt so perfect. So right.

Her hips rocked restlessly until she was riding against the hard ridge of his erection, the material of her panties and his jeans causing an absurdly delicious friction against her already-soaked flesh. Could he feel it? she wondered. The heat and wetness? She hoped so. Surely that spoke more eloquently to how much she wanted him than any words ever could.

God knew *her* words were never that eloquent.

His mouth slid down her neck and he bent to capture her nipple in his mouth. She gasped, then moaned at the tug of his lips, the swipe of his tongue. The empty ache between her legs intensified until it was within kissing distance of pain.

"Let's go to bed." His voice was low, rough, and she felt the words vibrate through every erogenous zone on her body. And as she was quickly learning, she had more of those than she originally thought.

Mischa practically leapt from his lap in her haste to get to the bedroom. The thought of feeling every inch of his flawless, caramel-colored skin against hers...

She shivered, then grabbed his hand, yanking him up off the couch to drag him to her bed.

Halfway there, in the middle of her hallway, he stopped. She groaned, glancing over her shoulder at him. "You're not going to change your mind, are you?"

But he looked like he hadn't even heard her. His dark gaze was taking a leisurely journey up her calves and thighs, lingering for a good long time on her cotton-clad backside, before trailing up her spine, across her shoulders.

She felt the weight of that gaze on every inch of her skin. Every. Inch.

"God, just look at this view," he murmured, awed.

His voice had a gravelly edge to it that made her gut—and a few other choice parts of her anatomy—clench with need.

"Put your hands on the wall."

The scent of lust in the air—his and hers—all around them intensified, erotic and ripe. Normally she would've questioned the request (demand, really), but at the moment, she was open to whatever he had planned, as long as it ended with him buried deep inside her.

She flattened her palms against the wall and gasped as he nudged her legs apart with his knee.

"Don't move," he whispered in her ear, his voice practically brimming with primal male satisfaction at the thought of having her at his carnal mercy.

He skated his fingers down her spine, over the curves of her ass, up over her ribs before moving to stand close behind her, mouth against her ear.

He combed his fingers through her hair, pushing it back away from her face. *Oh, please touch me*, she begged silently. Then, miraculously, he cupped her breasts.

She tipped her head back against his chest and moaned as he caressed her. He moved one hand lower, along the soft cotton band of her underwear, then lower still. It was his turn to moan when he discovered just how wet and ready for him she was.

Mischa pressed her hips against his hand in silent plea, and he gave her exactly what she wanted.

His fingers moved beneath her panties, and she edged her legs further apart so he could slide a finger through her slick folds.

"Yes," she murmured as he curled his other hand around her breast, rubbing his thumb over her nipple. "God, yes."

He leaned forward and kissed her neck right below her ear, a spot that never failed to make her shiver, and slid his finger inside her as he pressed his erection against her backside.

She bucked wildly against his hand, against his erection, and still he kept his rhythm deliberately, tortuously slow.

"Come now," he growled, lightly nipping at her ear lobe.

She shook her head, trembling harder, and he pressed a second finger inside her, rubbing his palm downward. She arched, crying out his name, and she felt her entire body tensing, bracing for orgasm.

"Can you feel how hard I am for you? How hard you make me?" He punctuated the question by pressing her back against his erection.

She moaned out something that might've been a "yes." She wasn't sure. She wasn't exactly coherent at the moment.

He must've approved of her answer, because he decided to answer her unspoken prayers, thrusting his fingers into her harder, faster, until her entire body jerked against him, and she let out a gasping cry before sagging against him, completely limp.

He had to wrap his arms around her in a tight hug to keep her upright. "Are you okay?" he whispered in her ear.

She shuddered again before mumbling something completely

unintelligible. He gently caught her ear lobe between his teeth and tugged. "Ready for round two?"

That got her attention. She looked up and over her shoulder at him. "Already?"

He laughed out loud at what must've been a look of stunned surprise in her wide eyes. "One of the best perks of being with a vampire, if you'll remember correctly, is stamina. And guess what?"

"What?" she whispered, still processing.

"You're a vampire now, too. Your stamina is just as good as mine. So, are you ready for round two?"

Oh. My. God.

She smiled at him, and his answering smile put the dawn to shame. "Bring it on," she challenged.

And with that, he tossed her over his shoulder caveman-style and strode purposefully toward her bedroom.

Chapter Twenty-four

Hunter tossed her on the mattress without preamble. She sprawled back on the bed, limbs visibly trembling with aftershocks from her orgasms, and shot him a slightly disgruntled look at being manhandled in such a way. Her expression darkened with lust and awe, though, as he quickly stripped off his pants and stared down at her, hands on hips.

If they both lived to be a thousand—which was, of course, a possibility—he'd never get over how pretty she was. Her curves, the smooth, golden skin, the deep, dark eyes, the little bow-shaped mouth…she was as close to heavenly perfection as he imagined he'd ever see. He knew in that moment he'd never get enough of her.

On all fours, he crawled over her until he reached her hips. The scent of their arousal—his and hers—mingled in the air, creating an intoxicating perfume that nearly drove him mad with the need to be inside her.

But not yet. Soon, though. This time when she came, he'd be buried balls-deep in her tight, wet heat.

He kissed her hip, the dip of her waist, moving up her ribcage with slow, gentle sweeps of his tongue. The soft, mewling little sounds of pleasure she made spurred him on.

She choked back a desperate moan as he traced the edge of her panties with his tongue.

"So beautiful," he murmured against her skin. "I lost hours, days, in prison thinking of nothing but this."

She wiggled desperately underneath him, and a moment later, her panties went flying across the room. "Please," she choked out.

"Don't make me wait anymore."

He lifted his head and smiled up at her. "As you wish."

The Princess Bride quotes were going to be the death of her. That is, if the slow, painful torture of waiting for him to be inside her didn't kill her first.

Finally, finally, he moved up, settling himself between her legs. It only took a second for him to begin sliding into her, slowly, eyes locked on hers.

The need to feel him filling her was more than she could stand. She raised her hips and looped her arms around his neck, urging him forward. Desperately she rocked against him, taking inch after inch of him until he was fully seated within her.

For a long moment, neither of them moved, just held themselves still, eyes locked on one another. Mischa suddenly felt bare, vulnerable. With him inside her, his eyes focused so intently on hers, there was nowhere to hide. Nowhere left to run. And for the first time in her life, she was happy to stay put.

He began to move, slower than she'd expected, but his face was beginning to show the strain of his efforts to hold back, to make it last for her sake.

"How can you feel better than I remember every time I'm with you?" he muttered, capturing her lips for another deep, wet kiss.

Goosebumps broke out along her flesh—*hey, I didn't even know vampires got those!*—as she rose to meet him halfway. With a growl, he slipped his hands under her butt and lifted so he could go deeper, each stroke putting the most delicious pressure on her clitoris.

Their moans melded, tongues tangled, bodies clashed over and over again until she felt adored and blissful, and tormented and battered all at the same time.

Mischa locked her ankles around his waist and arched beneath him as the pressure inside her built and built. He felt so good. So right. So...

"Mine," she whispered against his lips.

"Yes," he answered immediately. "Always."

That was pretty much all it took to break her. She screamed his name as she came, heard hers tumble from his lips on a hoarse groan as he followed her to completion.

It took about ten minutes of them lying together, coming back down to earth, before Mischa realized the ever-present hum of electricity was gone from her building...and on the streets.

Uh oh.

"Hunter, did you—"

"Yep," he said, gently nipping at her collarbone. "One of us—or both of us—shut down the power grid."

He didn't seem overly concerned about it, so neither was she. Until her phone rang.

She glanced over at the phone on her nightstand and saw it was Harper calling.

Uh oh.

Hunter reached over, grabbed the phone, hit the answer button and snarled, "She'll call you back later." He glanced down at her breasts and she felt him hardening inside her once again. "Much later," he added before hurling her phone at the wall.

"You'll pay for that later," she said lightly, not knowing for sure if she meant the shattered phone, or for ignoring Harper. With him inside her, looking down at her with such dark hunger in his eyes, it was hard to keep a coherent thought in her head.

"Later," he repeated, capturing her lips with his own. "Much later."

Chapter Twenty-five

Later—much, much later—Mischa lay sprawled, limp and sated, across Hunter's chest while he ran his fingers through her hair, making her scalp tingle most pleasantly.

"Can you tell me about prison?" she broached quietly.

He sighed. "There's not much to tell. If you want to know if I dropped the soap, I already told Harper I didn't."

She snorted. That sounded exactly like what Harper would ask. "No, that isn't what I was asking. When I saw you, that first night out, you had a bad cut on your cheek. Were you...in a fight?"

He was silent for so long she didn't think he was going to answer. But eventually, he said, "Yes. There were many fights."

There was pain in his voice. He did his best to mask it, but his time in prison had left marks on him, and not just the physical ones she'd seen when he was released. She couldn't make him talk about it, but...she had to know. She was the reason he'd ended up in that place to begin with. How could they move on together if she didn't understand everything he'd been through?

Her instincts told her not to do it, but she ignored them. Time to make Vi's advice *really* work for her.

Closing her eyes, she visualized the mental wall she'd had up in her mind for so long crumbling, toppling to the ground. Tentatively, she reached out with her mind, searching for his.

She gasped, feeling as if she was being pummeled with stray thoughts and voices, all speaking at once, some yelling, some rough and ugly. Moving her hands over her ears (which of course did no good, because the voices she was hearing were all inside her head), she shook her head, struggling for focus.

Pain lashed her temples like the crack of a whip against her flesh, but she gritted her teeth and fought through it, finally, *finally* managing to sort through all the voices—the memories and thoughts—she realized, until she found the one consciousness she was searching for.

Silver bars that burned into vampire flesh like a branding iron when touched. The stench of sweat and delousing spray and mildew from the walls seeping into your nostrils, into your skin. The noise—oh, God—the noise. Clanging metal and raised, angry voices and...hatred, sadness, violence everywhere. And the thirst...like lava eating a hole through your throat. Wracking, gut-wrenching hunger like he'd never known. Feral, snarling vampires everywhere, clawing, fighting, teeth snapping, tearing. This was hell...

"Mischa!"

Hunter gave her a hard shake and finally, his anxious voice jolted her back to reality, jerking her out of his memories where she'd felt like so much more than an observer.

When she managed to open her eyes and blink back the tears that filled her vision, he was sitting on top of her, thighs bracketing hers, hands on her shoulders, looking down at her with concerned eyes. "What the hell was that?" he yelled.

She cringed and covered her face with her hands. "I'm so, s-so sorry," she sobbed. "You never should have been in that place. I s-should have done more to get you out sooner. I—"

"Hey," he said, his voice gentling. "Stop that."

He repositioned them so that she was in his lap, curled up against his chest. "There wasn't anything you could've done," he said, resting his chin on top of her head. "I was there because I broke the law. I turned you without your written consent. I deserved my sentence."

She hiccupped loudly and would've been embarrassed if she wasn't so upset. "No one deserves what happened to you there. That place should be s-shut down."

"It wasn't really all that bad. The worst of it all came from one guard. And I doubt he'll be bothering any of the other prisoners from now on."

Yes, she'd seen that guard's face. Just because Hunter was willing to let him get away what he'd done—with his skin still attached to his body—didn't mean *she* was. She'd deal with him once their current case was solved.

"Wait," he said, "were you…in my head?"

She sniffled. "I'm sorry for the intrusion. I just…had to know what happened. And I got the feeling you were keeping it from me to protect me. I just—"

"Shh," he interrupted. "It's OK. Your…powers are strong for how young you are."

He did his best to keep the concern out of his voice, to sound neutral. But she heard it. The concern, the hesitation. "Is there any way to stop it?" she asked, almost afraid to hope.

He sighed again. "No. I'm sorry. I can help you deal with it better, though."

Mischa did her best to choke back a sob. Didn't quite manage it. An eternity spent knocking out the power grid and accidently controlling and reading peoples' minds was wholly unappealing.

Every fear and insecurity she'd ever had hit her all at once. Without his help…"I don't think I can do this," she whispered.

Hunter merely cuddled her closer and kissed the top of her head. "It's all right. Try to get some sleep," he said, his voice gruff. "You'll feel better tomorrow."

The good thing about emotional rock-bottom, as she knew from experience, was that he was right. Everything was always better tomorrow. After all, it couldn't get much worse, right?

Later, Hunter laid in bed, staring at the ceiling with Mischa cuddled up against his side, one leg thrown over his, her hair splayed across his chest. He should be happy, feeling nothing but contentment. This was, after all, exactly where he'd wanted to be for years. Two decades, even. And yet...

He was on edge. Off-balance. She'd always had this effect on him. But now, now that she was like him, it was worse somehow.

He'd lied before. Her powers weren't just strong for someone her age. They were strong for someone of *any* age. When she gained control? She'd be unstoppable. Stronger than him, even.

Her family tree must have a few...interesting branches, he thought. Only someone with magic in their blood when they were turned could gain the level of strength she had so quickly.

But that was a moot point if she never accepted her powers. It wouldn't be easy for her. She'd have to work harder than she'd ever worked to harness or contain that kind of strength.

And when things were at their darkest, when she was tired and didn't think she'd ever master the power raging within her...would she lean on him and let him help her? Or would she push him away?

I don't think I can do this.

That statement, in combination with her history of running, told him the odds were good that she'd push him away.

And now that he'd tasted heaven once again, would he be able to let her go if she ran again? A sick sense of panic rolled through him at the thought.

Mischa grumbled and squirmed in her sleep, and he realized he'd inadvertently tightened his hold on her.

He loosened his grip and stifled a self-deprecating chuckle. He grabbed her, she squirmed away. If that wasn't a metaphor for their entire relationship to date, he didn't know what was.

Chapter Twenty-six

Mischa jackknifed up in bed and flung an arm out to the opposite side of the bed. Her heart sank as her hand failed to meet smooth male flesh, instead landing only on a crinkly piece of paper.

Had to go help set up for the show tonight. We'll talk later.

Fuck! It had happened again.

Waking up alone totally sucked ass.

And, worst of all, it hurt her heart. She thought they'd really made progress this time. The sex, the apologies, the sex, the psychology tricks, all the talking, the *sex*...

"Son of a bitch!" she blurted to the empty room.

After everything they'd shared, everything she'd apologized for, everything they'd *done*, she'd never told him the most important thing. The only thing that really mattered at this point.

She'd never told him she loved him.

Well, hell, he must think...

She frowned, having no idea what he was thinking. But the fact that he'd left without saying goodbye—the note was beyond inadequate and unsatisfying—certainly couldn't be a good sign.

I don't think I can do this.

Holy shit! She'd actually said that to him! She'd meant that she wouldn't be able to do *this*, to learn to control her powers and be a vampire, without him. But since she hadn't been able to articulate that, he probably thought she meant she couldn't ever accept what she'd become. Or that she couldn't be with him.

Oh my God, I'm fucking this up again!

Panicked, she groped on the nightstand for her phone, only to belatedly remember that it was now in pieces on the floor.

"Shit!"

Jumping from bed, not bothering to put on clothes, Mischa ran at top vampire speed to grab her house phone. *Thank God the power seemed to be back up.* She punched in Hunter's number, waited, then growled when it went immediately to voice mail.

Taking a few unnecessary deep breaths in an effort to calm herself, she punched in the first number that popped into her mind after Hunter's.

"Breaker, breaker. Come on back, breaker."

Mischa glanced at the caller ID on her phone to make sure she'd dialed the right number. "What the fuck are you talking about?"

Harper sighed. "I'm bored. I'm watching *Smokey and the Bandit*. Sue me. What do you want?"

Yeah, this wasn't going to work with just the two of them. She was panicked and Harper was, well, *Harper*, so they needed a mature adult in the conversation.

"Hang on," she muttered, "I'm conferencing Vi in."

"Ten-four, good buddy," Harper answered around a mouthful of popcorn, by the sound of it.

Mischa face-palmed while she waited for Vi to pick up. About a hundred years later, Vi answered in her carefully cultured tones, "Dr. Violet Marchand."

"Vi, I've got Harper on the phone and I need help, damn it."

Vi's tone was bone-dry as she said, "I don't do therapy sessions over the phone with other people on the line, Mischa. No offense, Harper."

"None taken," Harper said, then belched. "Sorry. Baby's making me gassy."

Mischa chose to ignore that little tidbit and addressed Vi's comment instead. "I don't need a therapy session, Vi. I need advice from my friends."

She gave them the most succinct rundown of the night's events she could possibly give without letting too many personal (or naked) details slip. She wanted help, but didn't want to give Harper any ammunition for future teasing.

When she was done, Vi said, "Well, you screwed up again."

Harper added, "Yep."

Mischa's jaw clenched. "I know that! Now tell me how to fix it, damn it!"

"You're the worst apologizer in the world," Harper said. "Remember that time you backed into my car? You never said a word. The only way I knew it was you was that you kept bringing me food. For a month I was drowning in doughnuts, chocolate, and ice cream. Guilt food." She sighed happily. "Those were the days."

"Runners are always horrible at saying they're sorry," Vi added.

Jesus, she thought. These were her *friends*! She should've just called some of her enemies for advice. It couldn't have been much worse. "Fine," she ground out, "I'm the worst apologizer ever and I forgot to tell him I love him. I also might have implied that I was reluctant to continue our relationship. I fucked up. Fine. How do I make it right? He's not answering his phone."

Harper snorted. "He hardly ever answers that thing. And he won't admit it, but I don't think he knows how to pick up his voicemail. He sucks with technology."

"I've found that to be true with many of my older patients," Vi said. "The ones over, oh, two hundred or so never really seem to take to technology."

"Really? I always kind of thought they'd be happy to try, you know, considering how they grew up and—"

Mischa let out a snarl of frustration. "Can we discuss the technology habits of ancient vampires later and focus on, oh, I don't know, *me* right now? I'm freakin' losing my mind here!"

"OK, calm down," Vi said, adopting her best soothe-the-deranged-psychopath voice "Look, Hunter knows you pretty well. He's aware of your strengths and limitations and loves you despite—

and because of—them. I'm sure he wasn't expecting a stellar declaration of love from you."

Harper crunched a mouthful of popcorn before adding, "Yeah. And I wouldn't really worry about that note. Jesus, Riddick's monosyllabic half the time. Hunter's note to you was three times longer than any note Riddick's ever left for me, and it doesn't mean he's any less in love with me, you know?"

Mischa felt the knot in her chest loosen a bit. OK, maybe this wasn't as bad as she'd been thinking. Maybe everything was OK after all.

"Now, that doesn't mean you shouldn't tell him you love him right away," Vi advised. "Go find him. Be straight with him."

The knot tightened up again. "I tried that the first night he was back," she said, not caring that her voice had taken on a whining tone. "He said he wouldn't believe I loved him until I'd accepted what I am and learned to love myself."

"Oh, he's good," Vi murmured. "It took me a ton more words to say it than it took him. He's right, of course. Have you set yourself up with a blood donor? Have you contacted your family? Have you worked to gain control of your powers?"

Shit, she hadn't done any of that. And further, she'd asked him if there was any way to get rid of her powers.

Mischa let her forehead drop to her palm and let out a defeated groan. "Oh my God, I *really* screwed this all up again."

"This is what I'm saying," Harper garbled around a mouthful of popcorn.

"It's not too late," Vi soothed. "You can fix it. It takes five minutes to set yourself up with a blood donor. It can all be handled online. You can call your mom and ask to talk to her after the pageant. She'll understand. And as for the powers, well, you can always ask Hunter to help you with that. He's probably the only one who can, anyway."

Well, that all sounded…doable. "OK. I can do that. Then can I tell him I love him?"

Harper snorted. "I wouldn't just blurt it out. You've jerked him around too long for that."

"That's probably true," Vi murmured. "A grand gesture may be in order."

A grand gesture? What... "The fuck?"

"Time to hold your boom box up outside his house and blast some Peter Gabriel, Lloyd."

Of course. Leave it to Harper to explain the situation using an '80s movie reference. "A grand gesture. OK." Wow, creativity had never been her strong suit but she could figure this out. Or... "Have any suggestions?"

In the background, Mischa heard someone pronounce very distinctly, very slowly, "Show. Him. Your. Boobs."

You could almost hear Harper's eye roll as she said, "She's got it under control, Benny. Thanks, though."

"You gals always gotta complicate things," he muttered.

"We have to go," Harper said suddenly. "It's getting to the good part."

Mischa wondered briefly what exactly the "good part" of *Smokey and the Bandit* was, but thought better of asking.

Vi wished her luck and hung up as well, leaving Mischa alone with her thoughts.

So, all she had to do was solve the case, catch a crazed stalker who may or may not also be a murderer, come up with the perfect "grand gesture", and win back the man she loved, permanently.

What could possibly go wrong?

More things than you can count.

Stupid brain, she thought. Always being all...reasonable and shit. That just had to stop if any of her long-term plans were going to pan out.

Chapter Twenty-seven

Mischa decided that multi-tasking was her best bet, given the short amount of time she had left before the pageant that evening.

She decided to focus on the case first. After all, that was *way* easier to sort out than her love life.

She had Leon researching greenhouses and growers who might be capable of cultivating Kadupol flowers. If they were truly as fragile as Emily's research indicated, the stalker must have a greenhouse close by, or lots of cash on hand to get them transported quickly to Whispering Hope.

Benny was currently scouring hours and hours of pageant footage, as well as the hidden camera footage Hunter had set up, looking for anything, anyone, who appeared onscreen that looked out of place, suspicious.

Lucas had agreed—somewhat reluctantly—to run background checks on everyone who had registered to attend the swimsuit competition, in the hopes of finding anyone who might have ties to Emily and her hometown. The odds of him finding anything were slim. Pretty damn anorexic, really. But desperate times and all…

And on the personal front, Harper was setting up her online account with the blood bank so she could get regular deliveries of bagged blood, in case Hunter decided he didn't want to, um, donate to her anymore.

Just the thought of him not wanting to be with her anymore—blood donor or not—made tears spring to her eyes.

She gave herself a sharp mental slap across the face. "Focus, damn it," she muttered.

The one thing that was left on her to-do list for the day was the most difficult. And unfortunately, it wasn't a task she could delegate to anyone else. This one was all hers.

Settling on the bed, chewing her thumbnail, she eyed the new iPhone Riddick had picked up for her like it was the enemy. This was either going to go just-won-the-lottery fantastic, or just-got-hit-by-a-bus craptastic.

There was really no in-between with her family. Never had been.

She needed to do this. And not just to prove to Hunter that she was serious. She needed to set things straight with her family once and for all. If they didn't accept her as a vampire, so be it, but at least she could say she tried.

Gathering up every scrap of courage she had left, she dialed the number.

On the third ring, her mother answered.

"If you're selling something, I ain't interested."

Mischa couldn't help it; she barked out a laugh. "I'm not selling anything, Ma."

There was a long pause on the other end of the line, and Mischa could just imagine her mother, sitting on one of the barstools in her kitchen, cigarette between her fingers, cradling her old-fashioned, still-attached-to-the-wall corded phone.

"Is it my birthday already?" her mother asked dryly.

She deserved that. "I just needed to talk to you, Ma."

"What's wrong?" she asked, voice suddenly tight with tension.

Mischa bit off the rest of her fingernail and blurted, "I know the boys think I abandoned you when I left but I didn't, not really. I went to work for Sentry and they paid off all of Dad's debts. That money didn't come from a life insurance policy. It came because of me. And Dad didn't die in a car accident, he died from a vampire bite because he wanted to be turned. And I was hurt real bad six months ago and my boyfriend turned me into a vampire. Now I work for Harper and I track down vampires and…others who skip bail."

She could've gone on. After all, it's not like she had to stop to catch her breath or anything. But that was pretty much the whole story, she supposed.

There was another loaded, long pause on the other end of the line before her mother asked, "This boyfriend of yours…he's a nice Italian boy, yes? Catholic?"

Of all the questions she'd expected from her mother, she never could've guessed that one. "Um, no, Ma. He's Native American. Pretty sure he's not Catholic." Deciding to go big or go home, she added, "He's over five hundred years old."

"But he's good to you?"

Her stomach fluttered at the thought of how good to her he was. "Oh, yes. I love him, Ma."

A sigh. "Fine. Then it's settled. You'll bring him to dinner on Friday. Seven thirty."

Well, neither of them ate anymore, but her mother's tone brooked no room for argument, so she kept that knowledge to herself. But, still… "That's it? I spilled my guts and that's all you have to say? Your only questions are about Hunter?"

Over the line, Mischa heard her mother stub out her cigarette. "Well, baby, there wasn't much you told me that I wasn't already aware of. I mean, hell, I may not have your genius IQ, but I'm no dummy. I knew the money came from you."

Mischa sputtered. "How?"

"There was never a life insurance policy." Her mother snorted. "Every penny we ever had went into your dad's gambling. Even if there had been a policy—which there wasn't—he wouldn't have paid the premiums."

"And you knew about the…"

"Yes, yes. I knew about how much he wanted to be a vampire." Her mother tsked. "I always suspected that was how he died."

Mischa swallowed hard. "And you don't care that I'm a…"

"Let me tell you this, little girl," she interrupted sternly, "no matter what you are, no matter what you've done, I'm always on your side. You're my baby and I love you. End of story. And if this vampire of yours makes you happy and takes care of you, well, then I love him, too."

Mischa was afraid she'd start to cry if she said anything, so remained silent as her mother sniffed and added, "Even though it's a shame he's not Italian. I'll probably never hear the end of that from Maria Franchetti. You remember her daughter, Teresa, right? The little curly-headed girl with the impetigo? The one who used to pretend she was a dog and pee in the yard up until she was in the fourth grade? Well, she married an Italian doctor who is also Catholic. Canasta club has been unbearable since those two got engaged, let me tell you."

Mischa felt as if thousand-pound weights had just lifted from her shoulders as she listened to her mother prattle on about canasta club, who was doing what in the old neighborhood, and other hometown gossip.

Jesus, it felt so good to hear that her mother accepted her, even if Mischa had been having trouble accepting herself. But after the gossip session was done, she couldn't help but ask, "Ma, why didn't you ever say anything to me? About dad? About the money?"

"I assumed you'd tell me everything when you were ready. Even as a kid you were that way. Couldn't ever be rushed into doing anything. Had to do things in your own way, in your own time."

Mischa closed her eyes, not wanting to ask her next question, but knowing she didn't have a choice. "Do the boys…do they still hate me for leaving?"

"Those boys are every bit as stubborn as you are. They knew they were wrong to blame you for leaving, but do you think any one of them could admit it?" She snorted. "You don't worry about them for a minute. I'll talk to them. I think you'll be surprised at how quickly they'll welcome you back into the family with open arms."

A joy and giddiness she hadn't felt since, well, she couldn't even remember when, bubbled up within her. "Ma?"

"Yes, baby?"

"I love you."

"I love you, too."

Mischa added, quietly, "And I'm sorry I stayed away for so long. I was wrong."

Another pause. "Well, I'll just bet that hurt like the devil to say, didn't it?"

She chuckled. "You have no idea."

Chapter Twenty-eight

Hunter had absolutely no idea if he'd rigged the lighting for the final competition correctly. Harper had brought him in as a replacement for Riddick, who actually *did* know how to wire shit, but being able to carry the equipment and reading a book or two about stage lighting certainly didn't make him an expert. He'd been around two-hundred-sixty years or so before Ben Franklin even discovered electricity, for shit's sake. What did he know?

But, since a quick call to Riddick had confirmed that nothing he'd done was likely to start a fire, he decided to let it go.

"Should I not stand under the lighting, or are you nervous about something else?"

He glanced down from his perch on the lighting catwalk to see Tina, looking back up him through a pair of rose-colored glasses. And that wasn't a metaphor. They actually had rose-colored lenses and cat-eye frames, and they matched the scarf she had tied around her cloud of blond curls.

Hunter didn't claim to know anything about fashion, but even he knew Tina was rocking what could only be considered a vintage look.

Not bothering with the ladder, he dropped from the catwalk, landing in front of her almost silently. She shook her head. "Grace, good looks, and super powers. I'd hate you if you weren't such a sweetheart."

He was so thrown off by the "sweetheart" comment that he didn't bother pointing out that she herself was blessed with an abundance of grace, good looks, and super powers.

Then he remembered she'd asked a question, so he said, "The

lighting should be fine. How's Emily doing?"

She patted her hair and smiled up at him. "Oh, she's fine. She hit it off with my Michael, as I suspected she would. She's with him right now backstage, rehearsing her monologue for the talent competition."

He remembered Emily's voice from the interview portion of the competition, and the thought of her lending her squeaky, thin vocals to some kind of insipid dramatic monologue made him cringe. "That's...good. Any sign of her stalker?"

"Nope. Everything seems fine." Her gaze turned speculative. "So, if you're not worried about the lighting, I can only assume you're worried about...our girl?"

Worried wasn't the right word. Dreading the confrontation he knew they were going to have? That was accurate. And it would be a confrontation, of that he was sure.

He'd decided last night, while she'd slept so peacefully and trustingly in his arms, that he was done with the chase. She was either all in with him, or she was out. And if she was out...

Yeah, "worried" definitely wasn't the right word. Fucking terrified was more like it.

If she wasn't all in, if she didn't want him, complete with promises to love, honor and cherish until death (the permanent kind) do they part, he'd have to leave Whispering Hope. There was no way he could remain in the same town with the lost love of his life, possibly eventually having to watch her move on with someone else.

Just the thought made him want to disembowel this fictional man who would eventually win Mischa's heart. The smug fucker.

He shook his head. And Mischa thought *she* was twisted.

He'd never given her any kind of ultimatums before. He'd never demanded anything of her, knowing she'd have to make her own decisions in her own time. But now...well, he was demanding. It was time. They'd danced around each other for long enough.

Tina nodded as if she'd heard his entire inner monologue.

"Resolve. I can feel it. You're resolved to make a move. You're planning to tell her it's time to shit or get off the pot, yes? Help her get her shit together and force her to make a commitment?"

The unladylike turn of phrase was in direct opposition to her prim and pristine visage, and the statement was all the more powerful for it. He couldn't help but let out a choked laugh before saying, "Something like that."

She patted his shoulder, the gesture oddly motherly considering he was about, oh, several centuries older than her. "It's about time, dear. Don't worry about it. She's ready."

He fought the urge to press her for more information about how Mischa was feeling, lest he seem like a teenage girl gossiping with friends about cute boys. Time for a subject change. "Do you know what she plans to do for the talent competition?"

A commotion at the other end of the auditorium drew their attention.

In a brown leather La-Z-Boy recliner carried by Benny, Tiny, the bartender from the Rag Tag, and Leon, sat Harper, who had a bucket of fried chicken cradled against her stomach, and a Big Gulp Slurpee in her hand. She smiled brightly when she saw them and waved with a drumstick she'd just plucked from the bucket.

Tina's tiny hands fisted and shot to her hips. She sputtered as the men set the recliner down near the orchestra pit. "Child, what in the name of all that's holy are you doing here? You're supposed to be on bed rest."

Harper looked deceptively innocent as she said, "Well, technically, 'bed rest' is just a figure of speech. My doctor told me I had to 'recline' until I went into labor." Harper gestured to her chair. "Well, I'm reclining."

Hunter shifted his gaze to the men who'd just carried Harper in like she was Cleopatra atop her queen's litter. Tiny bent over at the waist, gulping for breath. Leon actually lay down on the floor at Harper's feet, his skin dotted with sweat and sickly pale. Benny leaned heavily against the recliner and cussed under his breath. His voice was too quiet for Harper to hear, but Hunter heard he was muttering something about pregnancy hormones and recliners that weighed more than circus elephants.

While Tina continued to sputter and stew, Hunter asked, "What are you doing here, Harper? Is something wrong?"

She gnawed off a huge chunk of chicken and shook her head. "Nope. Just wanted to see what Mischa came up with for the talent competition. I have a feeling it's going to be *epic*."

She balanced the bucket of chicken on her protruding belly and dug into the cushion of the recliner to pull out a small, hand-held video camera. "And I need to make sure it's captured for posterity."

Tina finally found her tongue and said, "You are just plain mean, Harper Hall. You think that girl is going to embarrass herself, and you want that video footage so you can torment her."

Harper's grin was delightful, cheerful, and terrifying all at the same time. "Yeah. Like I said: *epic*."

"I think," Leon said, panting, "I pulled my spleen."

"Suck it up, Buttercup," Harper barked like a Marine drill sergeant. "You can't pull your spleen, anyway. You'll be fine. Walk it off."

Tiny, Benny, and Leon excused themselves at that point, presumably to run for their lives before Harper asked to be moved elsewhere. She glanced around after they'd gone, taking in the scene, which included nervous vampire beauty pageant contestants milling around, practicing their acts for the talent competition (there seemed to be an inordinate number of vampires in the pageant with a talent for knife handling, for some reason), and chatting animatedly about the show, the previous day's attack, and…he listened for a moment…hair and makeup.

Harper whistled. "Wow, what a freak show."

Says the pregnant woman who was just carried in on a recliner by a halfer, a sleazy bar owner, and a computer nerd, he thought. The whole thing sounded like the setup for some kind of twisted joke.

Harper dug into the recliner's cushions again and handed Hunter a sheet of paper with a dozen or so names and addresses on it. "That's for Mischa," she said. "It's all the people in the country who are capable of cultivating and shipping Kadupul flowers."

He folded the paper and stuck it in his shirt pocket. "I'll make sure she gets it."

"Thanks. Now, can you move me back stage, on the right? I want to make sure I have the best camera angle for when—"

She was interrupted when the auditorium door banged opened. Actually, it sounded more like it was *kicked* open, Hunter thought. He followed the source of the noise and wasn't terribly surprised to see Riddick stalking toward Harper, murder in his eyes.

"Fuck," Harper muttered, then turned to her mother with accusing eyes. "Did you call him?"

Tina smiled sweetly, saying nothing, and tucked her phone back into her purse.

Riddick didn't stop until he was directly in front of Harper. She craned her neck back to smile up at him, guilelessly. "Hi, honey!" she chirped. "How are you?"

A muscle in his jaw twitched and his hands fisted at his sides. Her smile fell a bit. "I suppose you were worried when you got home and I wasn't there, huh?"

Worried was an understatement, if his expression was any indication, Hunter thought.

"I'm really sorry, but don't blame the guys, OK?" she said, biting her lower lip. "I made them bring me here."

Anyone who didn't know Harper Hall would say it was impossible that one tiny woman *made* those three grown men do anything. But, knowing Harper, it was a distinct possibility that they'd truly had no choice in the matter. She just had a way of making things work out to her advantage, which was kind of adorable…until it was used against you. Then it made you want to strangle her. Just a little.

Riddick opened his mouth to speak, then snapped it shut again. This went on two or three more times. Hunter felt for the guy. He'd certainly been reduced to mute fury a time or two when dealing with Mischa.

After another moment or two, Riddick gave up any pretense of carrying on a conversation with his wife. With a growl born of the purest frustration, he bent at the knees, picked up the recliner, turned on his heel, and stalked toward the auditorium's exit.

Hunter wondered idly if *dhampyres* could get hernias. The chair looked *that* heavy.

"Aw, come on, Riddick," Harper whined. "It's going to be epic! I can't miss this!"

When he didn't answer, she sighed and asked, "Can we at least stop for fries on the way home?"

Riddick kicked the door open and without so much as a backward glance, carried her—and her giant recliner—out.

Tina clapped her hands together. "Well, that was exciting. I'm off to check on Michael and Emily, dear. Good luck tonight!"

Yep. He'd take all the luck he could get at this point. He just hoped that if Harper was right and the evening was epic, her definition leaned more to the epically *good* than to the epically *bad*.

Chapter Twenty-nine

Tina sprayed enough old-school Aqua Net on Mischa's up-do to single-handedly create a hole in the ozone layer above their city. The intricate combination of braids and loose curls was most likely bullet-proof and hurricane-resistant. But, even Mischa (who barely brushed her hair most days) had to appreciate the results of Tina's efforts.

The style was classy while still managing to be fashion-forward. And she wasn't exactly sure how she'd done it, but Tina's make-up job made the most of her delicate features without looking like she was wearing anything at all. It was all so…artfully artless.

And her gown for the talent competition? There weren't enough adjectives in the English language to describe how much better she felt in it than she did in her swimsuit.

The dress was made of a rich emerald-green silk. It was low-cut in the bodice, slit on each side to mid-thigh, and it had been tailored specifically to suit her small frame. Somehow, it managed to be both elegant and erotic, revealing and classy all at the same time.

She supposed she owed Barbie an apology for assuming the woman would garb her in reams of pink taffeta and tulle.

Tina plucked a loose hair off Mischa's shoulder and met her gaze in the mirror. (And yes, vampires can see their reflections. Vampire movies were only about half accurate half the time.) "Are you sure you want to do this?"

Yes. No. Maybe. Probably…yes. No, definitely yes.

Tina chuckled. "Well, as long as you're sure."

Mischa let out a disgruntled groan. "I keep asking myself, 'what would Harper do,' you know? She's always so brave and confident.

But that doesn't really help here, because Harper wouldn't be in this mess to begin with."

Tina put her hands on Mischa's shoulders and turned her around so that they were eye to eye. (And for once, Mischa could actually *be* eye to eye with someone. They were the exact same height. It was a nice change of pace.) "Now you listen here, girlie. You need to stop doubting yourself once and for all. It's that doubt that got you into this mess to begin with. You're beautiful and smart and tough just like my Harper. But do you know what you have that she doesn't?"

Crippling indecision and bouts of pathological self-doubt? "No. What?"

"Quiet strength. The emotional kind. Now, don't get me wrong, Harper is strong. But she's fearless, too. Acts without thinking through consequences. It's easy to be strong when you're fearless. But you?" She shook her head and smiled warmly at her. "You think everything through. You're logical, methodical. So when you act? I know you do it with full knowledge of the consequences. And being brave and gutting something out when you fully understand the consequences? Well, there's nothing more terrifying than that."

Mischa swallowed hard against the lump that had appeared in her throat. "Harper's way sounds a lot better to me right now."

Tina gave her arm a sympathetic pat. "It almost always does, sweetheart. But this time, you've got nothing to worry about. That business about doing the opposite of what your instincts tell you?" She frowned and blew a raspberry. "I gotta tell you, no offense to your doctor friend, but that's a bunch of hooey. If I've learned anything over the years, it's that when you listen to your heart, it will never lead you astray. It's only the *mind* that can get twisted up and mess with you."

"You've got 5 minutes, New York! Move it to stage right."

Mischa and Tina both flinched at the stagehand's barked order. Tina scowled at him and in a razor-edged tone, said, "This beautiful young woman is not a lunch special, child. You can't just *order* her."

The stagehand opened his mouth to argue, but something he saw in her expression made him think better of it. After a moment, he mumbled, "My apologies, ma'am."

Tina sniffed delicately and removed her scarf, then slapped a hat down over her blond curls. She fussed with it for a moment before tilting it to a jaunty angle. "That's more like it." She waved an imperious hand in his direction. "Scuttle off, then. We'll be there in a moment."

When he was gone, Tina turned and gave Mischa's hair one last completely unnecessary spritz of hairspray. Under her breath, she muttered, "These kids today. I swear these video games and the internet have rotted their brains. Basic courtesy seems a foreign art to the little degenerates…now where were we? Oh, yes. Tell me, dear, what's your heart tell you need to do right now? Quick, without thinking."

"Go out there and take back what's mine," Mischa said, with zero hesitation.

Tina's answering smile was triumphant and reminded Mischa so much of Harper that she did a double take. "Well, then, what are we waiting for?"

Fuckin'-A, she thought, feeling a surge of confidence and resolve that she hadn't felt since…well, *ever* she supposed.

When Mischa reached her mark on the right side of the backstage area, Tina whispered, "Maybe this isn't the best time to ask, dear, but…can you actually sing?"

And *splat* went her confidence.

Son of a bitch. This was going to be as embarrassing as all fuck. Thank God Harper wasn't here to witness it.

Mischa traced the sign of the cross on her chest and stepped into the spotlight.

Chapter Thirty

I have seen things that cannot be unseen.

Wars, famine, heartbreak, tragedy…Hunter had seen it all. But what he'd seen today? Well, in its own way, the events of this day were every bit as horrifying as any atrocity he'd ever witnessed in his unnaturally long life.

He'd decided that the talent competition in a vampire beauty pageant was the lowest ring of hell. Lower than the bowels of Midvale prison. Lower than invasive surgery without anesthetic. Lower than a busy Saturday afternoon at Walmart.

Miss Delaware had performed interpretive dance to Bonnie Tyler's *Total Eclipse of the Heart*. Miss New Mexico had recited an original poem entitled *My Pussy*. Hunter thought it was about her cat, but the whole thing was ambiguous and…horrifying, so he tried not to overthink it.

Miss Wyoming did a dramatic reading from *The Notebook*, which might've been tolerable in and of itself. But since she chose to read the part of the male lead, the way she lowered her squeaky voice to imitate a man's deeper register somehow made the whole thing sad and unintentionally hilarious at the same time.

Then there was Miss Arizona.

He shuddered at the memory of the girl's ventriloquist act. Wasn't it universally understood that ventriloquist dummies were inherently evil?

And all the while, because he was in charge of the spotlight, he was forced to watch every mind-numbing performance until he wasn't sure who he felt sorrier for: the girl on stage, or himself.

But his mind completely blanked out as Mischa stepped onto the stage. She looked...like an angel. Her dress shifted as she moved, showing a whole lot of thigh on both sides.

A highly erotic angel.

With a grimace, she adjusted the microphone down to her height. (He was pretty sure Miss Arizona was part Amazon.) She closed her eyes and blew out in a way he'd seen humans do to calm themselves.

"I have to be honest with all of you," she said, her whiskey-smooth voice sending a shiver down his back. "I don't have any talent."

The audience laughed, and she chuckled right along with them. "Unless you count running, that is. Oh, I don't mean exercise. I mean running from my problems. Stuff that scares me. My life." Her smile turned into a half-smirk. "My death," she added, getting another laugh out of the audience.

"But being here, with everything that's happened lately..."

Hunter had no idea if she meant everything that happened in the pageant, or with the two of them since his release, but he was glad his job only called on him to point a light at her. He was too in tuned to what she was saying to do much else.

"...has made me realize I can't afford to run anymore. I've already lost too much because of it."

Her eyes glistened and it was all he could do not to go to her.

"I lost years of my life avoiding attachments. I messed up my relationship with my family." She cleared her throat. "And I pushed the man I love out of my life. But I'm going to do my damnedest to fix everything tonight."

"What the hell are you doing, love?" he murmured.

"I've already made amends with my family. They're all here in the front row. See?"

He aimed the light at the front row, and there was a tiny Italian woman, wildly waving and applauding, surrounded by eight young men who towered over her. Mischa's mother and brothers, he realized.

Moving the spotlight back to her, he shook his head in wonder. She'd actually done it. She'd made up with her family after twenty-plus years of estrangement.

"And now," she went on, shifting her gaze up to his, "all I need to do is win back the man I love. Trouble is, he won't let me tell him how I feel."

The crowd booed a bit, and Mischa quickly shushed them. "No, no. It's not his fault. I was a complete dumbass, trust me on that. But if he won't let me tell him how I feel, I'm left with no alternative but to sing it. I'll apologize to all of you in advance; this is most likely going to be horrible. So, without further ado, here it goes."

He recognized the music as soon as it started. His chest tightened as he listened to her sing the old Elvis song.

> *Maybe I didn't love you*
> *Quite as often as I could have*
> *Maybe I didn't treat you*
> *Quite as good as I should have*
> *If I made you feel second best*
> *I'm so sorry I was blind*
> *But you were always on my mind*
> *You were always on my mind*

"Well, it's not as bad as I thought it would be, at least," Tina whispered from directly behind him. "Her voice is no worse than Miss South Carolina. I swear to God, performing that song from *Titanic* should be illegal."

He had no idea how she'd managed to find her way up to the lighting catwalk in her ridiculous pumps and pencil-skirted suit, but he wasn't about to ask. All of his attention was focused on Mischa as she sang directly to him.

Tell me, tell me that your sweet love hasn't died
Give me, give me one more chance
To keep you satisfied
I'll keep you satisfied

Wait…she was saying way more than sorry, here. Did she mean…

"You know," Tina added, "she's the one who secured your early release."

He glanced back at her, shocked. "Who told you that?"

She scoffed. "Please. I don't need anyone to *tell* me that. Ask her if you don't believe me."

She would've had to do some serious maneuvering to make that happen. It wouldn't have been worth it if she didn't…

Turning his attention back to Mischa, he can't stop the stupid, lovesick grin he felt spreading across his face.

But you were always on my mind
You were always on my mind

Her voice wavered and broke on the last line, going thick with emotion. Those same emotions—relief and nervousness and anxious energy and pure, unadulterated love—read clearly on her face as she put a hand over her eyes, trying to shield them from the spotlight as she sought him out.

"Well, what the hell are you waiting for, you damn fool?" Tina hissed, swatting his shoulder. "Get down there!"

What the hell was he waiting for, indeed?

Flicking the spotlight off Mischa, he dropped from the catwalk, not bothering with the ladder.

Above him, he heard Tina sigh and say, "Oh, this is going to be good."

Chapter Thirty-one

The stage plunged into darkness, which shifted the energy in the audience (among the humans, anyway) from politely appreciative of her performance (which was every bit as appalling and pitchy as she'd feared it would be), to shocked murmurs and rumblings about what might be happening. Was it another attack?

And suddenly, without so much as sound of warning, he was right in front of her, close enough that she had to tip her head back to meet his gaze. "Hi," she whispered.

Hunter's lip twitched. "Hi."

She thanked God for her vampire eyesight, which allowed her to clearly see his expression, even on the pitch-black stage.

And then she immediately said another prayer of thanks that he didn't look embarrassed by her performance. Or ready to laugh at her.

"You know," she said, trying for a casual tone while feeling anything but, "I never believed in soulmates before. Not even when I was a little girl. I never believed I'd find anyone who was truly meant for me and me alone."

He hooked his fingers in his belt loops as he stared down at her, dark eyes carefully shuttered. "Is that so?"

She nodded. "It never seemed plausible, you know? I mean, the whole notion of people being drawn together and bound by fate? Pfffttt. Totally unbelievable."

His gaze shifted to her lips and her stomach fluttered. "Totally unbelievable," he murmured.

"But now I know," she whispered, nervous as all hell. "It's all true.

Now..."

"Now?" he prompted.

She swallowed hard. "It's you. You're my soulmate. You're...*it* for me. I've known since before you turned me, I just...couldn't admit it. Even to myself. It was all too scary."

His hands moved to her hips and he pulled her closer, squishing her breasts against his chest. Her nipples, of course, immediately went on high alert.

Mischa licked her lips and his eyes tracked the movement. But still he didn't say anything. She was pretty sure she was going to turn to dust and blow away on a breeze if he didn't say or do something soon, so she blurted, "I'm not afraid anymore. The thought of living without you is scarier than any possible rejection could ever be. I love you. So much."

"I know."

She blinked. Oh...kay. Not one of the possible replies she'd considered. "I...guess I deserved that."

He leaned in and cupped her cheeks in his hands. She saw a ghost of a smile on his face before his lips captured hers in a quick but thorough kiss. He pulled back to rest his forehead against hers and whisper, "I love you, too. Always."

His rumbling, growly voice warmed her to the tips of her toes. "Really? So, Harper was right? Humiliating myself worked?"

He gave her a small smirk. "The humiliation was a nice touch."

She would've given him a quick punch to the stomach for that one, but she was so happy she let it go. She closed her eyes and her knees sagged under the weight of her relief. But then it occurred to her that it was probably time to go big or go home.

"I can't guarantee I'm not going to fuck things up again," she said. Then she slapped a hand over her mouth. "Shit, I probably shouldn't say 'fuck' in case the mics are still picking this up." Then she closed her eyes and muttered, "And I probably shouldn't say 'shit' either. Ugh. I'm fu...messing everything up already."

He chuckled. "I don't give a fuck who might be listening. Go ahead and finish. I've been waiting forever to hear this."

Well, she couldn't argue with that. "I just mean that up until now, running has kind of been my thing. I'm not really good at sticking around. I'll probably make mistakes. But I'm going to stay in therapy, I'm going to keep learning about my powers, and if you don't want to, uh, feed me anymore, I've already arranged for a blood donor."

He growled. "The hell you're feeding from anyone but me."

His territorialism shouldn't turn her on, but it totally did. "My point is that I'm doing my best to…untwist myself. For you. For us. I still don't think I deserve you. But I swear that I'll never stop trying to do better. To *be* better. If you'll have me."

"If I'll have you?" He snorted. "You're all I've ever wanted in this world. If you hadn't pulled this stunt tonight, I'd fully planned on kidnapping you and keeping you tied to my bed until I could convince you to stay with me forever. I think we can safely say 'I'll have you.'"

Enough talking, she decided. She grabbed fistfuls of his shirt and yanked him down to her, crushing her mouth to his. She put every bit of emotion and love and hope she had into the kiss, feeling like her heart was swelling, pushing out all the insecurities she'd held onto her whole life. There was simply no room for that crap in her life—in *her*—anymore.

Suddenly the spotlight hit them once again and the audience went wild, hooting and hollering and cheering until the noise was nearly deafening. And still the kiss went on.

They broke apart only when the noise in the audience died down to hearty rounds of applause. Misha offered the crowd a little wave and guilty smile. She pointed to Hunter, mouthing to the audience, "This is him!"

Hunter laughed right along with the audience before sweeping her up into his arms and carrying her off the stage.

Above them, on the lighting catwalk, Tina dabbed at her damp eyes with a tissue she'd pulled from her bra and sighed happily: "I just love a happy ending."

Chapter Thirty-two

Real life sure had a way of bitch-slapping the hell out of a happy ending, Hunter thought.

His plans for dragging Mischa off to his bed and keeping her there for, oh, three or four hundred years, were thwarted when Barbie, the aptly named pageant organizer, frantically told the contestants that crowning the winner would have to wait until Miss Utah was found.

Harper's brother, who'd been backstage with Emily, Tina quickly realized, was also MIA. And Emily's dressing area? It was currently covered in Kadupul flowers that looked like they'd been stomped and methodically shredded petal by petal.

Violently damaged metaphor flowers, as Mischa had said, couldn't possibly be a good sign. Hunter tended to agree.

So now, they were backstage with a terrified Tina, as Mischa sat on his lap (he wasn't about to quit touching her anytime soon) scanning the list Harper had given him earlier.

"There's at least twenty people in this part of the country with the means to grow and transport these flowers," she murmured. "We don't have time to do background checks on all of them."

"We can probably eliminate the women, right?" he asked.

She nodded. "Theoretically. Unless he's using a woman as a front. But for the sake of argument, after we eliminate the women, that still leaves," she paused, doing a quick count, ticking off names with her fingertip, "twelve men."

Better than twenty, he supposed, but still not great. "What now?"

Mischa bit her lower lip, then reached into her cleavage to pull out her phone. He immediately went semi-hard. She twisted around to look him in the eye. "Really? Now?"

He shrugged, unapologetic. "My dick rarely cares about poor timing. It only knows a hot woman just touched her breasts."

Her pupils dilated, letting him know she wasn't completely immune to the lust he was feeling. "Oh. Well...hold that thought."

"Leon," she said into the phone, "I need a favor."

Whatever reply he made clearly wasn't what she wanted to hear, because she let out a frustrated growl that took Hunter from semi to fully hard in the span of a heartbeat. She jerked around to pin him with another surprised look. He shrugged again.

Giving her head a hard shake, she shifted her focus to the call and said through gritted teeth, "Leon, I realize you're busy and don't work for me, but this is really more a favor for Harper."

After listening for another moment, she muttered, "Yeah, of course you immediately agree in that case. I could probably ask you to spit-shine her toilets with your toothbrush and you'd agree. Fucker."

More silence as Leon snapped back with some reply. "Whatever. We'll talk about it tomorrow. Right now I need you to cross-reference the names of only the men on the list you gave Harper against who might have a green house or nursery here or within driving distance of Whispering Hope."

While Leon worked, Mischa explained, "If the stalker really did kidnap Michael and Emily, he'd need someplace safe and quiet to take them. And maybe he doesn't transport the flowers, but grows them close by? I don't know." Her posture slumped. "I'm reaching, here. I'm not a detective, for Christ's sake. I track down bail jumpers! Harper and Riddick usually figure this shit out."

Hunter ran his hand over her back in slow circles. "No, it makes sense. It's worth checking out."

Tina stopped chewing through her nails long enough to add, "I don't want Harper to know anything about this yet. Riddick's having a hard enough time keeping her at home. If she found this out, she'd be out of that bed and down here before you could spit. It wouldn't be good for her or the baby."

On that they could all agree.

"Yeah, Leon," Mischa said, then listened for a moment. "OK, can you text me the addresses? Thanks."

When she disconnected, she looked back at him. "There's a nursery about two hours from here that grows Kadupul flowers."

"It's...possible, I suppose." Although, he couldn't imagine a kidnapper grabbing two people, tossing them in a car, and driving *two hours* to his hideout.

Mischa rubbed the back of her neck with a weary sigh. "Yeah, I thought it seemed implausible, too."

He blinked at her. "I didn't say that. Not out loud anyway."

Her eyes widened. "Holy shit! I read your mind without even trying?"

It would appear so.

"It would appear so," she murmured, looking horrified.

Tina held up a placating hand. "OK, calm down. We'll work..." she gestured between them dismissively "...*all that* out later. Right now, we need to focus on finding my son."

"Right," Mischa said, seeming to get ahold of herself. "Right. So, the nursery, while implausible, should probably still be checked out. I'll let Lucas know. Maybe he can send some of his guys out there. The other name on the list doesn't make much sense, either."

"Why not?" Tina asked.

"Well, it's an old farmhouse out in the middle of nowhere. Leon said it hasn't been inhabited for years, but back in the day, the owners had a floral shop in town. They grew some of their more exotic flowers on the farm, then sold them in their shop. The owners died years ago, though."

"The Millers," Tina said. "Missy and Ellis Miller. There was a fire. Faulty wiring or something. The place was gutted. Missy and Ellis died in the fire. Their son survived, though. He went to live with his uncle in Utah in one of those crazy Mormon communities. His name was something unusual…something with an r, maybe." She pursed her lips and her brow furrowed. "Oh, shoot, why can't I remember it? It was almost British sounding. Missy was obsessed with Princess Di. Regal, maybe? No, that's not it…"

"Royal," Mischa whispered.

"Yes!" Tina exclaimed. "That's it. Wait…how did you know that?"

"Royal Janitorial is the name of the company Barbie hired to clean up before and after each event. We checked out all the janitors who came in, but we never checked out the owner. He could've borrowed any of his guys' credentials to get in and out of here as he pleased." She met Hunter's gaze with a wide-eyed one of her own. "This is it. He's probably got Michael and Emily out at the old farmhouse. And if we're lucky, maybe the former Miss New York and Miss New Jersey are there, too."

Hunter stood up and set her back on her feet. "I'll go. You stay here with Tina."

Her eyes immediately narrowed slightly, letting him know he'd inadvertently stepped in some shit. "There's no way I'm not going with you," she said, her calm voice belying the rising heat in her eyes.

Tina straightened to her full height and adjusted her little hat. "Me, too."

There were so many reasons why they shouldn't go with him. Tina was human, for God's sake, and wearing a ridiculous getup that would make moving quickly or quietly impossible for her. Mischa was strong, but she had little to no control over her powers, and any number of things could go horribly awry if she was scared or seriously stressed out in any way. He was best suited to handle this situation, and he could damn well do it efficiently on his own.

But something told him Tina and Mischa weren't interested in listening to reason on this one.

Mischa grabbed his arm and lifted big, beautiful, pleading brown eyes to his. "Michael's like a brother to me. I have to try and help. Please."

And just like that, he was a goner.

Pathetic.

He closed his eyes and pinched the bridge of his nose. Short of tying them up and tossing them in the broom closet—then facing Hell's fire and retribution when he finally let them out, which was a wholly unappealing idea—he saw no way to keep them out of this.

"So," he began, "there's nothing I can say to convince you to stay here, *safe and out of danger*, while I go and check out this farmhouse?"

"That's right," they said in stereo.

He muttered a foul curse under his breath before sweeping a hand out to let them pass. "Then lead the way, ladies. This should be fun."

Chapter Thirty-three

From the looks of the old farmhouse, there was little more than flaking lead paint and memories holding the place together.

Nature was waging war on the two-story house, fighting to take back the very land on which it was built. Poison ivy vines twined in and out of the cedar siding, wrapping around the crumbling stone of the chimney like a noose. Tiny saplings from the hundred-year-old maple trees in the front yard had taken root in the gutters, dragging them right off the house and to the ground in some spots.

Half the house had obviously been gutted by the fire that had killed the Millers, but it would appear the flames had spared the basement and at least part of the first and second floors.

The greenhouse behind what was left of the barn looked relatively untouched by the fire and nature. It looked perfectly capable of sustaining Royal's metaphor flowers of choice.

Mischa sniffed delicately. The scent of fear and desperation clung to the place like grim Death. They were definitely here.

Just off the main road, at the end of the quarter-mile long gravel driveway, Mischa sat in her car with Hunter and Tina, watching for any signs of movement in the house. "They're definitely in there," she murmured. "Michael and Emily for sure. And..." she sniffed the air delicately, then cringed at the one-two punch of mold and rotting vegetation she received for her efforts "...maybe someone else in the basement?"

Hunter nodded. "Two in the basement. Female. Vampire."

Well, hot damn, she thought. She'd found the missing contestants after all. Harper would be so proud of her.

If she also managed to save her brother from the sicko stalker, that is.

Tina squinted in the darkness toward the house. "I can't see a damn thing! How can you tell who's in there?"

Mischa lifted her upper lip a fraction to give Tina a glimpse of her fangs, then tapped her nose with her index finger.

"Oh, yeah," Tina muttered. "So, what do we do now? Storm the place?"

Typical response she'd expect from someone who'd given birth to Harper Hall. "No," Mischa said. "Not yet. I don't want to spook the guy, or take a chance that he'd have time to hurt one of them before we got there. Hunter, is anyone else in the basement?"

He closed his eyes for a moment, then answered, "No. Michael is on the main floor, in the living room. Emily and Royal are on the second floor."

Tina's voice wavered as she asked, "Is Michael...OK?"

"His heartbeat is strong."

For now.

Mischa gulped. Hunter hadn't said that part out loud, but she'd heard it clear as crystal. Michael was hurt. She glanced at the basement windows, then back at Hunter. "I'm pretty sure I can fit through those windows." She sent silent thanks to Tina for having the foresight to bring Mischa a change of clothes. The jeans, T-shirt, and ass-kicking boots were much better suited to breaking and entering than her pageant dress had been. "I can get the girls out while you go in after Michael. If we're quiet and fast, Royal won't even know we're in there."

He looked like he dearly wanted to object, but knew at this point, there really wasn't a better option. "All right. As long as we're quiet..."

But quiet—along with any hope they had of getting out of this mess with minimal bloodshed—went out the window when three police cars, sirens blaring, came screaming down the street. Maybe they were just driving by, she thought, fingers crossed.

Her heart sank as they one by one pulled into the gravel driveway. Uniformed officers popped out of the vehicles and drew their weapons…aiming at their car.

"Get out of the car with your hands up!" one of the officers barked.

"So much for quiet," Hunter muttered darkly.

"Oh, Christ on a donkey," Tina added. "What a complete clusterfuck."

Mischa couldn't have said it better herself.

Chapter Thirty-four

Clusterfuck didn't even begin to describe the sequence of events that occurred after the cops arrived on the scene.

The three officers, who Mischa now thought of as Larry, Curly, and Moe, were almost comical in their zeal to apprehend "the perp." She'd tried explaining the situation to them multiple times only to be screamed at and told to shut up, all with guns trained on them. At one point, Larry, who looked to be about twelve years old, said "Shut up, bitch," and roughly shoved her against the car to cuff her, to which Hunter took great exception.

And by *exception*, Mischa meant he flew into a terrifying rage the likes of which the young cops had never seen.

With an inhuman roar and a blast of power that crackled in the air around them like static electricity on steroids, he disarmed Curly and Moe, twisted their guns into pretzels—and in a particularly inspired move, he forced Larry to pistol-whip himself across the face. *Then* Hunter twisted *his* gun into a pretzel as well. And the really scary part?

He hadn't raised a hand to any of them. It'd all been done with nothing but the power of his mind and a few sweeping hand gestures.

Now, with Larry, Curly, and Moe on their knees with their fingers laced behind their heads, Mischa looked over at Hunter and whispered, "That was the coolest fucking thing I have ever seen in my life."

He gave her the crooked half-smile that never failed to weaken her knees. When this was all over, she was going to take him home, tie him to her bed and—

Tina batted at the air between them, nose wrinkling. "Oh, for God's sake, enough of that! This is a crisis!"

She was saved from making an embarrassed apology by Lucas's arrival. He got out of his car and took in the site of the officers at Hunter's feet, features tight with barely concealed rage.

Vi climbed out of the passenger's side, eyes wide behind her glasses and bouncing from Mischa to Hunter, then to Larry, Curly, and Moe.

"Vi, what the hell are you doing here?" Mischa asked.

Tina piped up with, "I asked Lucas to pick her up on his way here. He said WHPD doesn't have a hostage negotiator, and since we're dealing with a sicko vampire stalker and kidnapper, I immediately thought of Violet."

Violet pushed up her glasses with her index finger. "Yes," she said, tone dry as Sahara sand, "I'm your girl for sicko vampire stalkers and kidnappers."

Lucas paced in front of his officers, cussing and muttering under his breath like Yosemite Sam. "God damn it, you stupid motherfuckers. I specifically said to *hang back*. No lights. No sirens." He shoved both hands through his hair. "And instead, you come in hot, guns waving. It's like the fucking *Keystone Kops*."

The officers, still on their knees, grumbled apologetically, but Lucas wasn't having it. "If anything happens to Michael or the girls, I'll have every one of your fucking badges for this colossal fuck-up."

"Lucas, you might want to calm down," Mischa advised.

And it wasn't a suggestion based on the fact that he'd used some variation of the word "fuck" four times in two statements. Or the fact that scary veins were bulging out of his neck as he spoke. It was really more about his eyes.

They were glowing yellow.

He was about to lose control of his temper and shift into his wolf. In front of Larry, Curly, and Moe.

No one outside the paranormal world knew werewolves and

shifters existed. Sure, lots of people suspected. After all, since vampires came out of the coffin, people's minds had certainly opened up to all manner of paranormal possibilities. But werewolves and shifters hadn't come out publicly yet, and their communities might not appreciate it if Lucas outed them.

And last she heard, there were no other known paranormals on the WHPD payroll. It was likely that none of his co-workers knew he wasn't human. She suspected he'd like to keep it that way.

But he was apparently beyond rational thought, because his gaze shot to hers and a low growl rumbled in his chest.

Oh, no, he did not *just growl at me.* Mischa growled back and took a step toward him.

Hunter moved in front of her and held a hand up to Lucas. "I'd rather not kill you," he said calmly, "but I will."

A wet stain slowly spread across the front of Larry's pants as power—Hunter's and Lucas's—filled the air around them. Mischa couldn't blame the guy. There was a time when the sight of an angry ancient vampire would've made her pee herself, too.

"Leave now," Mischa said to Larry, Curly, and Moe in her most persuasive tone. They just blinked owlishly at her.

"You do better when you're frustrated or angry," Hunter said, eyes still on Lucas, who paced restlessly in front of them like, well, a wolf in a cage at the zoo. "Think about something that frustrates you and try again."

Honestly, that shouldn't be too hard, she thought. Mostly because the mere fact that they were here dealing with a sicko vampire stalker and kidnapper rather than at home, in bed, making up for lost time frustrated the holy hell out of her. Channeling that into her voice, she hissed, "Leave. Now."

The Three Stooges scrambled to their feet, piled into their cars, and tore out of there like someone had pushed a cosmic fast-forward button.

"Well done," Hunter said when they'd left, a hint of a smile in his voice.

"Thanks," she said, feeling rather proud of herself. "Now, Lucas, do you have control of yourself? Or do I need to tell you to leave, too?"

His eyes were slowly starting to shift back to their normal watery blue color, but his voice was still rough and grumbly as he said, "Your mind tricks won't work on me, Bartone."

Tina stalked over and swatted him on the nose with a rolled-up newspaper. "No," she said sternly, pointing a finger in his face. "Bad...werewolf."

Not even crickets could be heard in the stifling silence that followed.

The last traces of yellow bled from Lucas's eyes as he shifted his gaze down to Tina, who was still standing in front of him, clutching the newspaper in one hand, and tapping one dainty, high-heeled foot impatiently in the dirt and gravel beneath her.

"You hit me...with a newspaper," Lucas said, slowly, deliberately, like one might address a two year old.

"We don't have time for werewolf crap, Lucas Cooper. We're going to get my boy back, with or without your help. So you can either lead, follow, or get the hell out of the way." Tina punctuated her point by poking him in the chest. Hard.

"You. Hit. Me. With. A. Newspaper."

Tina narrowed her eyes on him. "Suck it up, Buttercup. Are you with us or not?"

Lucas rubbed his chest where she'd poked him. "Where did you even get a rolled-up newspaper?"

Vi blurted, "Well, it certainly didn't come from me. From my purse. If that's what you were thinking."

As all eyes turned to her, she gulped and leaned against Lucas's car as if hoping she could blend into the paint and disappear.

"I mean, why would I even have a rolled-up newspaper in my purse?" A high-pitched giggle seemed to claw its way out of her throat before she was able to choke it back. "It's not like I'd ever use it in my practice. If that's what you're thinking. I don't advocate..." she swallowed ... "violence of any kind."

Lucas snatched the newspaper out of Tina's hand and stalked to where Vi was cowering against the car. He stopped directly in front of her, but she kept her gaze stubbornly straight ahead, refusing (or unable) to meet his gaze, which put her eyes right about chest level.

"If I ever see this again, I'll assume its owner wants me to bend her over my knee and spank her with it," he said silkily. "In case that's what you were thinking."

The crazy hyena giggle escaped Vi's lips once again before she clapped a hand over her mouth to stifle it. She cleared her throat, still not meeting his gaze. "I'll just take this and dispose of it for you."

"That would be best," he said dryly.

Hunter chuckled and Mischa elbowed him in the ribs, fighting back a chuckle of her own.

Lucas turned back toward them, hands on hips, suddenly all business again. "OK, I'm with you. What do we know?"

"Michael on the first floor, the two missing girls in the basement, Emily and Royal on the second floor," Mischa summed up. "Oh, and our element of surprise? Yeah, that's pretty much fucked. Everyone for three counties knows we're here now."

Lucas cussed under his breath, but Hunter said, "And yet he didn't try and run. Maybe he's ready to end this."

Mischa swallowed hard. *End* just sounded so...final. Potentially deadly.

"What do you think, doc?" Lucas asked. "Think he's ready to end this?"

Vi adjusted her suit jacket and slipped easily back into professional mode. "His kidnapping of Emily and the destruction of the flowers is a break in his normal pattern, and demonstrates an anger with her that was never present before. I'm guessing that seeing her with Michael triggered the anger and possibly some feelings of betrayal.

So, to answer your question, I'm hypothesizing that yes, he's ready to end this."

"And by *end this*," Mischa began carefully, "I'm assuming you don't think he plans to turn himself in and let everyone go, right?"

Please say yes. Please say yes.

Vi's ensuing silence spoke louder than words ever could.

Mischa sighed. "Right. Okay, fine. I'll take that to mean we need to get everyone out of there before this escalates and gets out of control."

Lucas shook his head, looking disgusted with the situation and everyone involved. "I'll approach the house. Present myself as the hostage negotiator. See if I can find out what his plans are. What he wants. If he's at all reasonable, I'll try to get him to let Michael go as a sign of good faith."

He shoved his hands through his hair again—at this rate, he'd be bald by morning—and added, "Hopefully the fucker won't shoot me on sight."

"Regular bullets can't kill a werewolf, can they?" Vi asked.

He snorted. "No, but they sure as shit piss me off."

"This should be fun," Hunter said for the second time that night.

Mischa shook her head. "We really need to work on your definition of *fun*."

Chapter Thirty-five

Lucas's skills as a negotiator left a little to be desired.

It had all started off peacefully enough, but after about twenty minutes of talking, Royal flat-out refused to comply and let Michael go. Mischa couldn't remember every word that was said after that, but she knew that Royal hadn't appreciated being called a "pathetic blood-sucking psycho," or a "fuckwit parasite."

She was definitely going to recommend that Lucas take some anger management classes. If they all made it out of this clusterfuck, that is.

So now, Royal stood on the porch of his dilapidated crack shack with a forearm around Michael's throat and a gun at his temple. Hunter had suggested (using every bit of his power) that Lucas shut the hell up. So Lucas was currently sitting on the ground with his back against one of the maple trees in the front yard, rocking an impressive man pout.

Tina was practically digging a trench through the yard with her heels as she anxiously paced back and forth, shredding a tissue between nervous fingers. Vi had taken over hostage negotiations. But Mischa kept her eyes on Hunter, who was too quiet and intense-looking for her liking.

"What are you thinking?" she whispered. "It looks like you're doing math in your head."

"I am doing math in my head."

She frowned. "Like trig? Is this really the time?"

He narrowed his eyes as he continued to study Royal. "Just trying to determine if I can move fast enough to grab Michael before Royal can pull that trigger."

"And?"

"It'd be close."

"Close like if you forgot to carry the one, Michael's brains could end up on the front door of this house?"

He glanced down at her. "Pretty much."

She bit her lower lip. "I don't like things that close."

"Me neither."

"What about mind control?" she asked.

He shook his head. "He's got some good internal shields. Like you. And his guard is up right now. If I catch him when his guard is down, maybe then."

With everything that had gone on so far? Yeah, she wasn't counting on him letting his guard down anytime soon.

"So we're back to trying to negotiate our way out of this, huh?"

Hunter shrugged. "Vi seems to be doing OK."

That didn't really surprise Mischa. Crazed stalker or not, Royal looked like every nerd ever to grace a John Hughes film. Maybe an inch or two taller than Mischa with a slight build, unfortunate overbite, and freakishly large forehead, Royal was probably thrilled to be talking to Vi, in all her icy blond, classically pretty perfection.

But it was taking for-freakin'-ever. Seriously, Mischa was immortal and even *she* felt like she was going to die before this thing ended.

Hunter nudged her with his shoulder. "Michael has a bullet wound. Left upper thigh."

Mischa almost groaned at the reminder. Michael's blood smelled like brown sugar and melted butter. It was all she could do to try and ignore the untimely blood thirst the smell stirred in her. "I know. I can smell it."

"Notice how the smell has gotten stronger while he's been standing there?"

It had, she realized. Almost like…"Shit," she muttered as realization hit her right between the eyes.

"We need to end this quickly. He's losing too much blood."

He did look a little pale. And he seemed to be leaning back on Royal heavily for support.

Harper would never forgive her if she let anything happen to her brother.

Mischa turned and forced Hunter to look her in the eye. "Do you trust me?"

He frowned down at her. "Of course I do. You know that."

She snaked a hand behind his neck and dragged his mouth down to hers for a quick, hard kiss. "I just needed to hear it out loud. And I need you to remember it, because you're not going to like this."

Before she could change her mind, she turned away from Hunter and took a step toward the front porch. "I got this, Vi," she said. "Go over and sit with Lucas."

Vi's brow furrowed, but she nodded and did as Mischa asked.

"What are you doing?" Hunter asked, his voice taking on a razor-sharp edge.

Forgive me, she thought, before turning to Royal and saying, "Michael's not looking so good, Royal. If you kill a human, you'll have the WHPD and the Vampire Council all over you. Let him go."

He sneered at her. "So your ancient boyfriend over there can mind-fuck me into turning myself over to the cops? No thanks. There's no way I'm giving up my hostage."

Yeah, I thought you'd say that.

She swallowed hard. "I'm not asking you to give up your hostage. I'll take his place."

Chapter Thirty-six

Royal was, of course, all too willing to rid himself of the bleeding liability of a human in his arms in exchange for Mischa, the vampire who all but trounced his beloved Emily in the Miss Eternity pageant.

Hunter grabbed her arm and spun her around to face him. "Are you fucking insane?" he hissed. "I'm not letting you hand yourself over to that sick fuck."

Her expression was maddeningly calm as she grabbed his hands, lacing her fingers through his. "I don't want to go either, but we don't have a choice. Michael will bleed out if he has to stand there much longer. He won't take you or Lucas in exchange for Michael because you could overpower him. I won't let him take Vi because she's every bit as vulnerable as Michael. He'll underestimate me because I'm small. I might be able to get him to drop his guard long enough for you guys to take him down."

Or maybe she could use her powers on him, she was thinking.

His hands tightened reflexively around hers. "Don't even think about it. Your powers are still too unreliable. If something went wrong..."

If something went wrong and you died, I'd destroy Royal, this house, everyone inside this house, and maybe everyone in this city. There's no one who could stop me.

"I feel the same way," she whispered in response to his unspoken confession. "But we don't have any other options."

"We'll figure something out."

"Give me an hour," she urged. "I'll give you a signal if I'm able to gain control. If you don't get a signal, you can storm the place."

Storming the place sounded pretty good. But not with her inside at the mercy of some sicko.

"He's not a killer," she went on. "I can see it. He didn't kill those girls in the basement. He could've. And he hasn't killed Michael. It's not his intention to kill me. I believe that."

He dropped one of her hands to shove his fingers through his hair in frustration, only to realize that it had yet to grow back from his prison-issue buzz cut. He growled. "He tried to kill you onstage."

"We don't know that. He could've just been trying to scare me."

"Well, it scared the holy hell out of me!"

She captured his hand again and pressed it to her heart. "I deal with dangerous and unpredictable every day in my job. This isn't all that different."

"I hate that fucking job," he grumbled.

"I know you do. But I'm good at it. Let me do this. Give me an hour. I'll be fine. Please. Please trust me."

"Goddammit." He squeezed his eyes shut. The "please" had always been his undoing with her. And she was right. They didn't really have any other options. No good ones, anyway. "You have *half* an hour. If I don't get a signal from you in that time letting me know you have everything under control, I will rip this place apart and kill anything that stands between us."

She smiled and pushed up on her tiptoes to press her lips to his. "Thank you. You won't regret it."

"I already do."

When Hunter was right, he was dead-on-balls accurate. Going in alone had been a stupid move.

Mischa didn't want to open her eyes. God only knew what was waiting for her beyond the quiet of her forced nap.

The whole thing had gone down quickly. She remembered Royal shoving Michael down the porch steps into Hunter's arms, then grabbing her upper arm and propelling her into the house. He'd slammed the door behind them and knocked her over the head with something blunt and heavy. She'd only had enough time to mutter, "Well, fuck," before her vision had dimmed to black and her body hit the floor.

"Is she OK?" a frightened voice whispered.

"I don't know," another answered. "Who do you think she is?"

"No idea. She's too short to be another contestant."

Well, that hardly seemed called for.

Mischa slowly raised her head and looked around the room, the light from a bare bulb screwed into the ceiling stabbed into her brain, making her hiss with pain.

They were in what looked to be the kitchen of an abandoned apartment. The basement, she realized.

The rotting remains of a farmhouse sink base cabinet leaned crookedly against the decaying wall. The smells of decades old mold and mildew filled the air, causing her nose to twitch. The peeling linoleum beneath her butt was a sickening shade of '70s avocado green and reminded Mischa of the time she'd had the flu as a child and puked up lime Jell-O.

Across from her were the former Miss New York and Miss New Jersey. Their arms and legs were bound with silver, and they were chained to the old galvanized pipes that jutted up from the floor. The women were dirty and disheveled, but otherwise seemed unharmed.

"My name's Mischa," she told them. "Let's see if we can get you out of here."

She briefly explained her role in the investigation to find them, the hostage crisis currently unfolding upstairs, and Royal's role in it all.

Miss New York hissed. "I knew that uppity bitch from Utah would be a problem. I'm reporting her to the Council when I get out of here."

The more reasonable Miss New Jersey said, "Oh, come on. It's not her fault the guy's a crazy stalker."

"It's her fault she never told the cops about him."

Mischa had to agree on that one. But they didn't really have time to discuss that topic in detail. "How long was I unconscious?"

Miss New York shrugged, but Miss New Jersey said, "No more than a couple of minutes. He must've thought being tossed down the stairs would be harder on you than it was. I mean, he didn't even bother chaining you up."

No, but being tossed down the stairs would explain the ache in her ribs and the bruise she could feel forming on her butt.

"Time to get you out of these chains," she muttered, crawling across the floor to them.

"We already tried to break them," New York said. "There's no way you can do it. You're too young."

She yanked their chains from the wall, the locks crumbing to dust under the pressure of her hands.

"Holy shit," New York muttered, eyes wide. "You been drinking Popeye's blood or something, little girl?"

No, just the blood of the oldest known vampire in the state. Maybe the country. No biggie.

She glanced at the small, cracked basement windows. "Can you guys squeeze through one of those?"

New Jersey snorted. "You'd be amazed at what I'm willing to try after being trapped down here for weeks."

"No shit," New York agreed. "Are you comin' with us?"

Mischa shook her head. "I'm going after Emily."

New York frowned. "She doesn't deserve your help. This whole thing is her fault. Come with us."

"I'll be fine. Don't worry about me."

New Jersey tugged her into a big bear hug before disappearing out the window faster than Mischa could blink. New York hesitated, poised to squeeze through the tiny window. "Be careful, OK? He hasn't hurt us, but he's gotten noticeably more unstable over the past day or so. I'm not convinced he won't try to kill you if you come between him and what he wants."

Mischa nodded. "Oh, by the way, when you get out there? You'll see a really dangerous, nervous-looking guy waiting for me. Will you tell him I'm OK?"

New York gave her a little half-smile before disappearing into the night.

"All right," Mischa muttered out loud. "Three hostages out, one to go."

What could possibly go wrong?

Chapter Thirty-seven

As a human, Mischa had always been a little clumsy. Harper had once said she sounded like a baby elephant tromping down the hall. But now that she was a vampire? Pfffttt. She was like a freakin' ninja!

She'd managed to get herself out of the basement and make her way up the rickety stairs to the charred remains of the farmhouse's second floor without making a sound.

Now, she slid down the hall with slow, steady steps until she was right outside the bedroom where Royal was holding Emily.

"Stop crying!" Royal screeched. "I've given you everything you ever wanted. I gave you *immortality*. And you sit there crying because I let your little human boy toy go. How about a little *fucking gratitude* for everything I've done for you?"

Thank you for stalking me, said…no one. Ever.

So Royal had turned Emily. Interesting. Mischa wondered if he'd set up the accident that killed her, too.

"I never asked you for anything," Emily choked out.

"No," he answered, a sneer in his voice. "You were too dumb to ask for anything. You just blindly took what I offered you. Did you really think I'd never ask for anything in return?"

There was a long pause. "What do you want?"

"We're leaving this place," he said. "Tonight. You're mine, Emily. Your little pet human can't stop me."

Emily just cried harder.

It was the sound of flesh smacking against flesh and Emily's startled gasp that jolted Mischa into action. The bastard had hit her!

With one well-placed kick, Mischa knocked the door right off its hinges and into a stunned Royal, who tossed the door aside and glared at her, confusion and shock and anger swirling in his black eyes.

"I knew I should've chained you up with the others," he muttered.

She shrugged. "Wouldn't have done you any good. Apparently it takes more than a few lousy silver chains to stop me."

His eyes widened, then narrowed. "You let the others go, didn't you?"

"Yep."

He shook his head. "I didn't want to have to kill you."

She inched forward ever so slightly, eyes on his hands, which clutched a jagged-edged hunting knife in a white-knuckled grip. "Well, that works out fine for me, because I don't really want to die."

"I said I didn't *want* to have to kill you. Not that I wouldn't."

He lunged for her, and Mischa aimed her best kick at his wrist, knocking his knife across the room. She pulled her 9mm out of her waistband and tried to aim, but he was too fast for her, and she got a sharp punch to the kidneys for her efforts. Her gun went flying. She lashed out with her foot, catching him in the knee. The resulting crunch gave her a certain grim satisfaction.

"You bitch!" he snarled, coming for her again.

"Get out of here!" she shouted at Emily.

But Emily was too far gone to listen, curled up on the bed in the fetal position, holding her hands over her ears and crying like a little girl.

If she lived through this, Mischa was totally going to spend some quality time smacking some backbone into Emily.

Time to try another tactic.

"Get out of here," she said again, shoving as much of her power as she could into the words.

And just like that, Emily stood up and started making her way slowly out of the room.

"And stop sniveling," Mischa added, gratified when the girl finally pulled herself together and disappeared from the room.

Huh. Getting used to her vampire powers might be easier than she thought.

Royal howled in frustration and made a move to grab Emily, but Mischa stopped him by slamming the heel of her hand into his nose, which was an effective little move Riddick had taught her.

Royal grabbed her shoulder and yanked her forward. She used her momentum and head-butted the bastard.

Harper had taught her that one.

"Fuck!" He tossed her away from him so hard the back of her head slammed into the wall and she slid to the floor.

Her vision blurred and the room tilted a little. Shit. That couldn't be good. Could a vampire get a concussion?

Royal loomed over her, blood covering his face and dripping down onto the front of his white button-down. He swiped at his swollen, obviously broken nose with his sleeve.

"I.Am.Going.To.Fucking.Kill.You."

"No, you're not."

Mischa's eyes widened as the newcomer made his presence known. Hunter filled the doorway, his eyes lighting with an almost feral glow as they took in the sight of Royal standing over her. His power filled the room, crackling and as intense and elemental as an electrical storm.

Apparently her hour was up. She almost felt sorry for Royal.

Almost.

Royal turned and the two men circled each other in slow motion.

"You know, I could peel your skin from your body as easily as peeling an orange and never lay a hand on you to do it," Hunter began, his tone sounding casual, calm. "But that wouldn't be as much fun as beating you until you can't stand, then stringing you from the ceiling from your own entrails."

Royal swallowed hard, looking nervous for the first time. Mischa was getting kind of nervous herself. "Hunter, I'm fine. There's no reason to...disembowel anyone."

"You're bleeding," he said without looking at her. "He hurt you. He dies."

Royal lunged forward with a frantic snarl and they clashed in a blurred tangle Mischa could barely track, even with her enhanced vision.

It was bloody and violent and horrifying to watch. The sounds of fists pounding against flesh, breaking bones, and pained grunts filled the room. They were locked together, fighting to the death, and Mischa could only watch it all in mute horror.

But as quickly as it had started, it was over, with Royal face down on the ground, arms twisted and mangled, laying uselessly at his sides. Hunter had his knee in Royal's back, his hands twisting Royal's neck back at an impossible angle. One twist and Hunter would rip Royal's head clean off his shoulders.

And end up back in prison for committing cold-blooded murder. The Council didn't look kindly on recidivism.

"Hunter, you have to stop and let the police take him in," she said urgently, grabbing his arm. "You'll go back to prison if you kill him."

The muscles beneath her fingers bunched and tightened. "It'll be worth it," he said through obviously clenched teeth.

Mischa let go of Hunter's arm and ran her fingers over his short hair. "Don't leave me again," she whispered. "Please."

He made a noise like a trapped beast and closed his eyes. "You just had to say 'please,' didn't you?"

She laid her head on his shoulder and smiled when he let go of Royal's head to slip an arm around her waist. "I'll make it up to you later."

"You'll pay for this," Royal sputtered. "I'll see that you pay—"

Mischa brought her booted foot down his head, swiftly, without hesitation, silencing whatever threat he'd been planning to make.

Hunter pulled back and raised a brow.

"What?" she asked. "He'll live. I never said he had to be *conscious* when the police took him."

He shook his head, the expression in his eyes somewhere just shy of total adoration and awe. "I love you."

She grinned. "I know."

Chapter Thirty-eight

"So, the bastard's already shot me in the leg, he's got the gun to my head, and I says, 'Go ahead and kill me, mother fucker! Just don't hurt my Emily'."

Hunter didn't recall hearing Michael say anything like that during his ordeal, but he saw no reason to rob the boy of his hero moment.

Emily cuddled up against Michael in his hospital bed and all but purred, "Oh, honey, you were so brave! What would I have done without you there?"

She would've stayed curled up in the fetal position on the bed, blubbering and about as useful as an appendix, Hunter thought.

Next to him, Mischa smothered a laugh with a fake cough. He grinned down at her. He'd never been with anyone who was able to read his thoughts. It was weird, definitely. But strangely intimate and comforting as well. It meant their bond was strengthening, and as far as he was concerned, it couldn't get strong enough for his liking. He wanted her in every aspect of his life. He was hers, body, heart, and soul.

She looped her arms around his waist and laid her head on his chest. He tightened his arms around her and kissed the top of her head, wishing they were at home, alone.

Naked would be good, too.

But naked alone time wasn't in the cards just yet.

Michael's hospital room was full to capacity. Tina sat in a chair at the head of the bed, alternating between offering to get her son something to eat, and fluffing his pillows and tucking his blankets around him like she probably did when he was sick as a child.

Harper—and her brown recliner—sat at the foot of the bed. Riddick (who must've carried that stupid chair out of their apartment, to the hospital, then up to the fifth floor) stood behind the chair, arms crossed over his chest, eyeing the hallway warily, as if they could be attacked at any moment. *Dhampyre* protective instincts, Hunter immediately recognized. Hunter could relate.

"So I'm confused about why Royal tried to kill Mischa," Harper said, hand protectively rubbing her belly.

"Well, when Lucas took his statement, he said he hadn't tried to kill anyone. He took a shot at me hoping to scare me into quitting the competition," Mischa said.

"Why not just kidnap you like the others?" Emily asked.

Mischa tightened her hold on his waist. "Apparently, once he realized I was a threat, I was never alone long enough for him to grab me."

"And he probably realized she could kick his ass," Hunter added, chuckling at the memory of Royal's busted nose. Before he'd shown up, Mischa had done a number on the stupid bastard.

"What are the odds that he'll lawyer up and get out of the charges?" Tina asked.

"Oh, according to Lucas, he's already lawyered up," Mischa said. "His business is worth millions, and he has all the right connections on the Council to get him out of serving jail time."

Emily's eyes widened. "He's going to get out?"

Mischa nodded. "He's claiming Michael's gunshot wound was an accident. That in combination with the fact that I wasn't really hurt and the other girls weren't really hurt means the Council will most likely let him slide with a big whopping 'donation' to the Council elders. But, the good news is that they've already agreed to wipe Royal's memory of Emily and all things Whispering Hope before his release. So he shouldn't bother any of us ever again."

"Shit," Michael said. "They're powerful enough to do that?"

Mischa glanced at Hunter. "No. But they have a volunteer who is."

Hunter's smile at the thought of having Royal at his mercy could only be described as feral. Apparently, the memory-wiping process wasn't exactly…pleasant.

Harper gasped and leaned forward in her seat, brow furrowing.

Riddick moved faster than a human could ever move and kneeled in front of her. "What is it?"

She smiled, but it was a tense echo of her usual smile. "It's nothing. Baby's just kicking."

Tina rubbed her own stomach. "That wasn't just a kick. That really hurt."

"Ugh!" Michael exclaimed. "That's gross, Ma."

"I can't help it!" Tina cried. "My leg's been aching something awful since you got shot, too. I can't block out what my babies are feeling."

"Well, try harder," Harper said through gritted teeth. "Michael's right. That's just weird."

Then she held up her hand, skin slowly draining of color, and asked, "Wait, you can't feel it when I'm having sex, too, can you?"

"Jesus," Riddick muttered, looking nauseated.

Tina looked thoughtful. "I don't think so. But I suppose I probably could if you were doing it, say, in my house while I was home, or something. I wonder if…"

Michael grabbed a puke basin off his bedside table and dry-heaved into it while Harper and Tina bickered back and forth about boundaries versus scientific curiosity.

They were all completely insane, Hunter realized. And because Mischa was part of their family (an honorary member, but still), he would be dealing with this group of crazy people for decades to come.

He waited for horror to settle in. It didn't.

Huh. Go figure.

He smiled down at Mischa and opened his mouth to joke with her about her certifiable adoptive clan, but snapped it shut abruptly when he saw the look on her face.

"What's wrong?" he asked.

She closed her eyes and canted her head towards Harper. "Everyone be quiet."

Her tone brooked no argument. Everyone shut up immediately.

A moment later, she looked up at him with wide eyes. "Do you hear that?"

He shifted his focus to Harper and listened. At first, he heard nothing but the flow of Harper's blood through her veins, the push and pull of air in and out of her lungs. But then…

"Yes," he murmured.

"Is that…normal?" Mischa asked.

He didn't know if she was asking if what she'd heard was normal, or if the fact that she could hear it at all was normal. Didn't really matter, he supposed. The answer was the same either way. "Um…no."

Harper couldn't hold her tongue any longer. "What the fuck is going on? What do you both hear?"

Mischa went over and laid her head on Harper's stomach.

Harper blinked down at her, nonplussed. "OK, this isn't weird or awkward at all."

Riddick looked ready to tear the room apart with his bare hands. "Someone better tell me what the fuck is going on right the fuck now."

Mischa ignored him and looked up at Harper, eyes wide. "I hear her."

Emily gasped and Tina crossed herself, muttering, "Jesus, Mary, and Joseph."

Michael shook his head. "You've always been a weirdo, short round. But this is fucking weird even for you."

Harper groped blindly for Riddick without taking her eyes off Mischa.

He grabbed her hand, looking like he'd been hit between the eyes with a two-by-four.

"Her?" Harper whispered. "It's a girl?"

Mischa nodded and let out a watery laugh. "It's time. She's ready."

Riddick growled. "No fucking way. It's too early. She's not due for another month."

Hunter shook his head. "She's strong. Heart, lungs, brain...she's definitely ready."

"How is that possible?" Tina asked, lower lip trembling.

"Well, Riddick's DNA is...advanced," Hunter answered. "And Harper's psychic, so she's obviously got some magic in her blood. It's not terribly far-fetched to think their baby wouldn't need as much time to develop as a normal human baby. Leon could probably give you a more scientific reason."

As a former Sentry biochemist, Leon was probably more qualified than anyone to tell her why the baby was ready early. But as far as being able to make *sure* the baby was ready? Mischa had already done that.

Mischa looked up at Riddick. "Get your doctor. Now. The pains she's been feeling? Those are labor pains."

He went three shades of pale before running out of the room like it was on fire. Hunter hoped he remembered to actually speak to the doctor before dragging him back to Harper's room by his or her hair.

Harper grabbed Mischa's hand. "Do you understand now about your powers? They're nothing to be afraid of. You can save lives. You can *help* people. It's a *good* thing you are the way you are. Just like Riddick, just like my mom, just like me."

"I think I *finally* understand," Mischa said quietly.

Harper winced and squeezed Mischa's hand as another labor pain hit. "Well, thank Christ for that, because I don't think I have time to explain it to your dumb ass. Oh, I almost forgot. Will you be the baby's godmother?"

Mischa swallowed visibly. "Are you...are you sure?"

Harper grinned at her. "Are you kidding? You're like a sister to me, and besides that, you're a vampire with super powers. Who better to protect my baby if I'm not around to do it? Hunter, you're up for godfather, too, if you're in. And don't worry, I won't make you do a Brando impression. Yet."

Well, this was a first, he thought. He'd walked the earth for over five centuries and no one had ever asked him to be part of their family or entrusted him with anything so precious. It was…humbling.

Leave it to Harper Hall to humble an ancient creature such as himself.

He gave her the only answer he could possibly give when faced with that kind of great honor. "I'll protect her with my life."

Chapter Thirty-nine

Two hours later, Haven Marie Hall was born.

Weighing in at an impressive nine pounds, eight ounces (which might explain why her mother had such an unfathomable appetite over the past few months), Haven was every bit as ready to face the world as Mischa and Hunter had said she'd be.

And now that she was out in the world, neither Hunter nor Mischa could hear her thoughts anymore, which meant she already had some instinctive, powerful mental shields. It appeared that little Haven, like her mother, would never be boring.

Harper had named her daughter in honor of her maternal grandmother, which had made Tina bawl uncontrollably for about ten minutes. She'd most likely depleted her entire supply of bra tissues.

Mischa had asked Riddick why Harper and Haven hadn't taken his name. He'd simply shrugged and told her that three Riddicks in the world (meaning him, his father, and the sister he'd never met) were more than enough, and his girls deserved better than that kind of legacy.

Having seen Riddick fight his ruthless father, a fellow *dhampyre*, in the supernatural equivalent of *Fight Club* the previous year, Mischa couldn't really dispute the truth in his words.

As for Riddick's sister, though...well, Mischa guessed they'd cross that bridge when they came to it. Maybe she was more like Riddick than their father. Fingers crossed.

But looking at Riddick, sitting in Harper's hospital bed with his wife leaning back against him, their beautiful baby girl nestled lovingly in her mother's arms, it was clear that his father and sister were the last things on his mind.

Mischa leaned back against Hunter, who immediately wrapped his arms around her waist and rested his chin on the top of her head. "I don't think I've ever seen anything this beautiful," she whispered quietly, so as not to disturb the new family.

"I have," he whispered back.

In his thoughts, she caught a quick flash of her face as she writhed beneath him and called out his name. She shivered, hoping to relive that particular memory sooner rather than later. "You're comparing me coming to the miracle of new life being brought into the world?"

"You're the only miracle I'll ever need, love," he answered simply.

She turned in his arms and looked up at him. "We never really talked about this, and I have no idea how you feel about it because you weren't exactly raised a Catholic like me. But I want what they have," she said, gesturing to Harper and Riddick. "The whole thing, starting with marriage. I know it's crazy and irrational since I'm not all that religious anymore, but…I want to stand up in front of friends and family and promise to be true to each other forever."

One corner of his mouth kicked up in her favorite crooked smile. "I don't suppose this would be a good time to tell you we're already married."

She couldn't help it. Her jaw dropped. She probably looked like a simpleton as she stared up at him. "We're *what* now?"

"By vampire law, we're married. Mated, in vampire terminology. It happens when you exchange blood and claim each other. You know, the whole 'mine' thing?"

Mischa blinked up at him a few times before she could put together a coherent thought. "So…you didn't think that was something you should tell me earlier?"

"I wanted to tell you, but you were so…"

"Twisted," she finished for him.

He nodded. "It's an antiquated tradition, anyway. I wouldn't have held you to the marriage if you decided you didn't want to stay with me. I didn't see the point in bringing it up at the time. And then everything with Royal happened, then Harper…"

She got it. Their timing had been off. Again.

"And if you would've let me go," she said, ignoring the pain in her chest that came along with that thought, "what about you? Would that mean you wouldn't be able to ever choose another mate?"

He looked confused. "Why would I ever want to choose another mate?"

Best. Answer. Ever.

Mischa grabbed him by the back of the neck, dragged his mouth down to hers and kissed the hell out of him.

She was definitely irked he hadn't bothered to tell her they were married. But even if he had, would anything have changed? No way. She still would've had to come to terms with her feelings all on her own. But still…

Mischa pulled back and punched him in the stomach.

He grunted, but didn't let go of her. "What was that for?"

"I just realized the public humiliation was *totally* unnecessary. We were already married, for Christ's sake! No more keeping secrets from me, got it?"

"Got it."

He said it seriously enough, but his eyes were clearly smiling, so she pointed her index finger at him. "And we're still getting married the human way. You're not getting out of that, mister. You're going to stand there in that church in a tux—" she paused, taking a moment to imagine the yummy goodness that was Hunter in formal wear, "—and we're going to promise to love each other forever, got it?"

"Got it."

"Well…all right then."

"You're going to have to get married here," Harper said from behind them. "I'm out if you're going to Vegas."

"Fucking Vegas," Riddick muttered.

Since she'd died there, Mischa couldn't see herself ever returning to Vegas, even if Elvis himself turned up and wanted to give one last performance at the Bellagio. Then another thought occurred to her.

"Do you think…do you think vampires are ever allowed to adopt children?"

Hunter looked thoughtful. "Between the two of us? I don't think there's anyone we couldn't convince to let us adopt."

"Not even the Council?" she asked, scowling on the word "Council."

"The Council is made up of the strongest vampires who want the job," Hunter reminded her. "If they were to say no to you and you—or me, for that matter—happened to want a place on the Council, there's no one there who's strong enough to challenge us."

Behind her, Harper said, "Shit. Looks like I'm about to lose a skip-tracer."

"We'll hire another," Riddick said in his usual bored tone.

Mischa ignored them, suddenly feeling like everything she'd ever wanted in her life was now within her grasp. Like she was slowly…untwisting. The old Mischa would've been scared at this point. Been sure the tide would inevitably turn against her. But the new Mischa?

"Can we get married next week and take over the Council right afterwards?"

Hunter gave up the pretense of looking serious at that point and smiled so big and beautiful it made her lightheaded. "As you wish, love. As you wish."

The End
(But stay tuned for Lucas's story, coming in 2017)
And in case you missed them, keep turning the pages to find excerpts from books 1 & 2 of the Harper Hall Investigations series,
***Semi-Charmed* and *Semi-Human*!**

A personal note from Isabel:

If you enjoyed this book, first of all, thanks! It would mean a lot to me if you would take a moment and show your support of indie authors (like me) by leaving a review on Amazon or Goodreads. Your reviews are a very important part of helping readers discover new books.

Want to know more about me, or when the next book release is? You can email me directly at: isabel.jordan@izzyjo.com. Also feel free to stalk me on:

Facebook: https://www.facebook.com/SemiCharmedAuthor
Twitter:@izzyjord
Website: http://www.izzyjo.com/

Thanks so much, and happy reading!

Sincerely,

Isabel

In case you missed it, here's a sneak peek of *Semi-Charmed*!

Whispering Hope, New York, today

Harper Hall swatted the fast-fingered hand of yet another horny, middle-aged CPA off her ass, but resisted the urge to dump tequila in this one's lap. After all, the Prince Valiant haircut and underbite he was saddled with were punishments enough for his crimes.

"Hey, baby," Valiant's friend said as he fondled his shot glass suggestively. "Is that a mirror in your pocket? 'Cause I can definitely see myself in your pants."

Harper rolled her eyes and shot back, "Darlin', I'm not your type. I'm not inflatable."

And with that, she turned on the heel of one of her requisite six-inch platforms and started for the bar as the CPAs chortled and bumped knuckles. They were probably looking at her butt too, but Harper chose not to dwell on that, or on the fact that most of said butt was probably hanging out of her Daisy Dukes. Not her best look, to be sure.

Lanie Cale, one of the other waitresses, grabbed her arm and leaned in, shouting over the music, "Hey, can you take over for me with the guy at table five? Carlos is letting me dance tonight. I go on in ten."

Harper gave her a quick once over. Lanie was five years her junior, ten pounds lighter, and had her beat by a full cup size. If she was Lanie, she'd probably aspire to be a stripper too. But as it stood, she was stuck waiting tables with the other B-cups.

"Sure," she answered. "But, Lanie, this guy at table five...he's not a CPA, is he? I don't think I have the strength for another CPA."

"No way is this guy a CPA. I'd bet Hugh Jackman's abs on it," she promised solemnly as she disappeared into the crowd.

At that moment, the sweaty throng of dancers and customers and waitresses parted, giving Harper her first glimpse of the guy at table five.

Wow. Hugh Jackman's abs were in no danger tonight.

The guy at table five was definitely *not* an accountant. Serial killer, maybe. CPA...um, no.

Table five was wedged in the corner, to the *extreme* right of the stage, which was why no one usually wanted to sit there. But instinct told Harper this guy had refused to sit anywhere else. This was one of those never-let-anyone-sneak-up-behind-you types, maybe with a military or law enforcement background. Paranoid and probably with good reason.

Everything about him screamed tall, dark, and brooding. From the black hair long overdue for a trim to the black-on-black wardrobe, complete with biker boots and a *Highlander*-like leather trench, this guy was either a true rebel without a cause, or the best imitation of one she'd ever seen.

And he was drunk off his ass. Not the kind of happy, silly drunk the CPAs at table ten had going. No, Harper could tell by the way he was ignoring the half-naked dancer on stage that he was drowning his sorrows.

Ignoring Misty Mountains wasn't easy, either. Her brand new double D's were mesmerizing, and the nipples kind of followed you wherever you went like the eyes on the creepy Jesus picture in her mom's living room.

As Harper watched, he polished off a bottle of Glenlivet and set it beside two other empties. She sighed. He'd probably pass out before he remembered to tip her. God damn drunks would be the death of her.

Harper squared her shoulders and walked up to the table, then knelt beside him so he could hear her over the baseline of Bon Jovi's *Lay Your Hands On Me*.

"Can I get you anything else, sir? Like coffee?" *Hint, hint.*

He didn't even glance at her as he slid the empty bottles to the edge of the table and said, "Another bottle."

His voice sent a shiver down her spine. It was gravelly, raspy, almost like he'd growled the words instead of speaking them. *Sexy*.

But sexy voice or not, she wasn't about to serve him another bottle. He was probably a few inches over six feet and maybe a little over two-hundred pounds, but no one--not even a manly man like this one--could down four bottles of eighteen-year-old Glenlivet and blow a Breathalyzer that wouldn't get him immediately arrested.

"I think you've probably had enough for tonight."

He slowly glanced over at her as if he hadn't really noticed her presence until just then. When her eyes locked with his, she completely forgot what they'd been talking about. Hell, who was she kidding? She forgot how to *breathe*.

This had to be the most gorgeous potential serial killer she'd ever seen.

He had a dark olive complexion most women would kill for, cheekbones sharp enough to cut glass, and eyes that were either black or the deepest blue she'd ever seen--it was too dark in the club to tell for sure.

His perfectly arched black brows--and they had to be naturally perfect, because she was pretty sure this guy wouldn't be caught dead waxing--raised sardonically as his gaze moved over her.

Harper fought the urge to suck in her stomach and desperately wished her uniform was a size eight instead of a four. She had dignity in a size eight. Class, even. In a four...not so much.

He lowered his gaze to her chest, and then slowly lifted it back to her eyes. "I doubt they're paying you to think, sunshine." Sliding the empty bottles even closer to her, he repeated, "Another bottle."

He'd said it very slowly, deliberately, in a manner most people reserved for slow-witted children and foreigners. The only part of her that wasn't at all impressed with the guy's fallen-angel face--which just happened to be her Sicilian temper--kicked in at that point.

Harper straightened and snagged the bottles off the table, preparing to verbally flay him, but just when she'd figured out exactly how many four-letter words she could hurl at him in one sentence, a premonition hit her hard.

People often asked her what premonitions felt like. Imagine someone punching a hole through your forehead and making a fist around your brain, she always told them. This premonition was no different.

Harper staggered forward and planted one palm on the table to steady herself as images assailed her: a young, blonde woman in an alley pinned to a dumpster by a man twice her size.

A vampire, she knew instinctively. Cold chills always shot down her spine when she saw them.

Harper sucked in a deep breath and forced herself to concentrate on details other than the victim, just like Sentry taught her so many years ago. Instead, she tried to picture the dumpster, the buildings around it, street signs…anything that might tell her where this girl was so she could call the police and get her some help.

And then she saw a logo printed on the side of the dumpster as big as life. *Kitty Kat Palace.*

Holy shit, the vamp and his victim were *here.*

Like it so far? You can download your copy right here: http://amzn.to/2b8AS9d

In case you missed it, here's a sneak peek (well, more than a sneak peek, really, it's the whole first chapter!) of *Semi-Human*!

Whispering Hope, New York

Harper Hall never thought she'd receive a marriage proposal while straddling a vampire stripper on the floor of the Kitty Kat Palace.

The stripper in question was named Candy Kane, which, unfortunately for her, was her real name. She'd been arrested a few weeks ago for illegal use of vampire mind control and was released on a twenty-thousand dollar bond. She failed to show for her court appearance. That's when she became Harper's problem.

Ah, the glamorous life of a paranormal PI.

Skip tracing, or tracking down bail jumpers, was Harper's least favorite kind of case. Bounty hunters and other PIs didn't want to go after vampires because they *always* resisted being brought in, resulting in all kinds of fucked-up, fang-y asshattery.

Hence her current position straddling Candy's face-down, prone body, which she'd pinned to the sticky strip club floor—*eeewww*—with her weight.

Sadly, skip tracing paid twice as much as any case she'd ever had, so she found herself doing it with disturbing regularity of late. Riddick seemed to enjoy it, though, given the semi-feral gleam in his eyes at the moment.

Her partner, Noah Riddick, had just slammed Candy's boyfriend face-first into the wall and wrenched his arms behind his back with enough force to break a normal human's bones. Fortunately, Candy's boyfriend, a real charmer by the name of Big Willy, was also a vampire.

And having had the, uh, pleasure of seeing the all-vampire male review he put on at the brand new show club—Vamp Me—in downtown Whispering Hope, Harper could truly say he did the Big

Willy moniker proud.

Apparently, Candy and Willy planned to rob patrons at the Kitty Kat Palace by way of Candy's mind control. By the time she was done with the hapless losers who requested lap dances, they'd think it was *their* idea to hand their wallets and phones and car keys over to Willy.

What they hadn't counted on was the bar's owner, Carlos Mendoza, calling Harper the second Willy hit the door.

Carlos would tell everyone he ratted out Willy and Candy out of concern for his patrons, but Harper knew he was probably just pissed off that the Bonnie and Clyde wannabes hadn't offered him a cut of their earnings.

"Get off me, you whore!"

Harper pressed her knee down harder against Candy's spine and wrenched the vamp's arms up higher behind her back to still her wild squirming. "Those who live in glass *whorehouses* shouldn't throw stones, sister," she said. "And I'm not the one pinned to the floor of a strip club wearing nothing but a set of heart-shaped pasties and a bedazzled G-string."

She glanced over at Riddick just in time to see Big Willy throw his head back toward Riddick's face in an attempt to break his nose. Riddick neatly avoided the head-butt, grabbed a fistful of Willy's shoulder-length, dishwater-dull blond hair and slammed the vamp's face into the wall.

Willy groaned. "You broke my fucking nose, asshole!"

Only it sounded like, "Ew boke my fuckin' bose, ash hoe," which made Harper giggle.

Riddick shrugged and recaptured Big Willy's arms, binding his wrists behind his back with a zip tie. "I told you to stand still or I'd start breaking your bones."

"I didn't do anything wrong, man."

Harper rolled her eyes. "Yeah, right. Did you forget I'm psychic, Willy?" She tapped her temple with her index finger. "Past, present, and future, all up here. And as soon as I touched your girl here I saw everything."

And when she said "everything," she meant *everything*. Not only had Candy and Big Willy robbed patrons at every strip club within a hundred-mile radius of Whispering Hope, they also had a very…*active* sex life. She'd seen things she was pretty sure weren't legal in most states. And some that seemed to defy physics.

"You can't prove anything," Willy said petulantly.

"No, but I'm pretty sure there's a reward for anyone who has information on the strip club robberies, which, *I* now do."

"Fucking bitch," he muttered.

The words had barely left Willy's mouth before Riddick kicked him in the back of the knee hard enough that bone and cartilage snapped and cracked. Willy screeched like a little girl and fell to the ground, clutching his temporarily ruined knee. It would take a young vampire like Willy at least a week to heal an injury like that.

Harper frowned at Riddick. "Was that necessary?"

He nodded. "I feel pretty good about it."

"You could've given him a warning."

"That *was* my warning."

She sighed. Riddick's protectiveness occasionally bordered on obsessive. She'd told him repeatedly that she could take care of herself, and breaking someone's bones over a little name-calling wasn't necessary. But he just couldn't seem to help himself.

She supposed it was romantic…in a psychotic sort of way.

Then he smiled at her, and her consternation vanished. Her heart kicked into an irregular, giddy rhythm that might've worried her if it didn't happen every time he flashed that sexy grin at her.

And the way he looked at the moment didn't exactly help slow her heart rate, either.

His thick black hair fell to his collar in careless disarray, giving him a just-fucked look that made her thoughts lean toward dirty, dirty things. He had the kind of lean, toned body that screamed badass instead of gym rat. And his face...

Fallen angels *wished* they had a face like Riddick's.

And he was all hers.

Suck it, other women everywhere!

"Let me go," Candy commanded, her normal Betty-Boop voice an octave lower than usual.

Harper tightened her hold on Candy's arms. "Don't embarrass yourself. Mind control doesn't work on me. Strong with the force am I," she added in her best Yoda voice, which was really kind of awful, now that she thought about it.

Note to self: no more Yoda voice.

"Don't bother trying it on him, either." She tipped her head in Riddick's direction. "He's immune, too."

Riddick gave her a mock bow as Willy continued to writhe on the ground at his feet.

Candy tipped her head to the side and glared up at Harper out of the corner of her eye. "I remember you two now," she hissed. "You worked for Sentry. You're murderers!"

Murderers is a little harsh, Harper thought, feeling vaguely offended.

Harper had been recruited by Sentry when she was just a kid. The psychic visions she'd been "gifted" with were a great asset to the organization. They allowed slayers to get the jump on vampires and other paranormal threats to humanity. And threats were eliminated with extreme prejudice. Until vampires came out of the coffin, that is.

About seven years ago, when vampires earned human rights, public backlash had shut Sentry down. No one liked the idea of a covert government agency putting vampires down like rabid dogs, so ex-Sentry employees were often met with prejudice and disdain these days, especially by prospective employers (hence her glamorous current gig).

And as if that weren't bad enough, since then, Harper had spent enough time with vampires to know that like humans, they weren't *all* bad, as Sentry had led her to believe most of her life.

She'd no doubt be judged one day for her actions—no matter how misled she might have been by Sentry. But she'd be *damned* if a thieving little wench like Candy would be doing the judging.

A muscle in Riddick's jaw twitched, letting her know he didn't like Candy's little reminder about Sentry, either.

Riddick had been a slayer for Sentry—but not just *any* slayer. His strength, speed, and hunting ability hadn't come from Sentry-administered drugs, as it had for other slayers. Riddick had been born with his talents.

According to Mischa, her BFF who'd worked for Sentry as a watcher, natural-born slayers were no better than wild animals: unpredictable, untamable, deadly if provoked. Riddick struggled every day to keep his inner beast in check and remain in control.

And for the most part, Willy's shattered knee notwithstanding, he succeeded. He was her partner. The guy who'd helped her triple the agency's business over the past year. The guy who'd saved her life. Twice. The guy who always let her have the last piece of pie. The guy who held her while she slept every night, all night, even though he could only sleep about four hours at a time.

The guy who was an absolute *God* in bed.

And in Harper's experience, men who knew their way around a clitoris *and* a G-spot were rare animals indeed.

"Sticks and stones, sweetheart," she said lightly. "Call me whatever you want, but don't insult him or I'll make what he did to your boyfriend's knee look like a love tap. I've been authorized to bring you in using *whatever* force is necessary."

Which was a total lie, but Candy didn't need to know that.

"Oh, you're in luuuuvvvv." Candy sneered. "How pathetic."

"Yep. And you're going to jail mostly naked. Who's pathetic now?"

That shut her right up. Thank God.

"Hey, Riddick, do you have an extra zip tie?"

What a stupid question, she thought as he reached into his leather trench coat. The man was a walking arsenal. He had everything from silver knives and short swords to zip ties, cuffs, and duct tape on him at all times.

Her hand brushed his when she reached for the tie, and a vision hit her right between the eyes. Harper pressed her hands to her temples, letting the vision roll over her.

She waited to see the usual vampires and blood and death, but they never came. Instead of some random victim, this time Harper's vision was of…well, Harper.

She stood on worn red velvet carpet at what looked like an altar. An old man in an even older suit stood before her, holding a Bible. Next to her was Riddick. They looked happy, if a little (okay, a lot) dirty and disheveled. And just as Riddick moved to slide a ring on her finger, the vision faded.

"God dammit!"

Riddick knelt beside her, looking concerned. "You okay?" he asked.

She blinked away the remnants of her vision. "Yeah," she said after a short pause. "It was just a vision."

"Meditation stopped working, huh?"

Her friend Hunter, a vampire who was so old that—if you got him drunk enough—he'd tell stories about what a pompous jerkoff George Custer was, had been helping her learn meditation techniques to control her visions. It had been working, for the most part. Nine times out of ten these days, she could channel her energy into avoiding moments when random contact with other people sparked a vision, which allowed her to trigger one herself when she really needed it (like during work hours).

Hunter had warned her that it probably wasn't going to be foolproof, though, since psychic gifts were unpredictable by design. She supposed this incident proved he was right.

"That was the weirdest thing I've ever seen," she told him.

He raised a brow, looking shocked. It had been a pretty bold statement, she realized, considering some of the freaky shit she'd seen over the years.

"That bad, huh?"

Harper shook her head. "No, not bad at all. But…"

Riddick brushed her hair off her forehead. "But what?"

Her mouth went dry. Could she voice this out loud without sounding like a crazed girlfriend pushing her guy for a forever kind of commitment?

She shuddered. God, that even sounded pathetic in her head. "Well…I thought I just saw…us…getting…"

Beneath her, Candy groaned. "If this is a sex story, let me be the first to say *eeeewwww*."

Harper smacked her in the back of the head with an open palm. Riddick took the zip tie and bound Candy's wrists, probably a little too tight based on Candy's grunt. But at least she shut up.

"You saw us getting what, Sunshine?" Riddick asked, still looking concerned.

"Ummm…*married*."

He paled a little at the word, and Harper instantly panicked. "Not that I'm pressing you, or anything. I mean, we've only been together for a year, and we've never even talked about marriage, so I *totally* get that what I just saw probably wasn't right, and—"

Riddick cupped the back of her head and yanked her toward him for a hard, fast kiss. When he pulled back, she was speechless. Well, except for the little gasp/moan combo that escaped her lips.

He rested his forehead on hers, fingers still wound in her hair. "I know you're not pressing me. I just didn't want to ask you like *this*," he said, gesturing with his free hand to the vampire beneath her.

"Holy shit," she murmured. "You really *do* want to marry me?"

Candy turned her head toward Riddick. "Really? *Her?* You're way out of her league, cheekbones. Murderer or not."

They ignored her.

Riddick flashed her favorite sexy half-smile, and if she'd been standing, she would've wobbled. "Are you kidding? Why wouldn't I want to marry you? You're smart and sexy and just dropped a vampire twice your size to the floor without even breaking a sweat. You're a fucking goddess."

Candy sniffed. "I'm not *twice* her size. I'm just bigger-boned," she said, sounding offended.

Harper's head was swimming. She hadn't had much luck with marriage. Her miserable cheating bastard of an ex-husband still might have a restraining order out on her, come to think of it. Did she even *want* to get married again?

Riddick cupped her jaw and brushed a tear she didn't even realize she'd shed away with his thumb. "I know I don't deserve you. Not even by a long shot. And I don't have a thing to offer you but me…and let's face it, I'm pretty well and truly fucked up."

She let out a watery chuckle and his eyes crinkled up at the corners a little with his answering smile.

"But if you'll have me," he added, "I'm yours. There's no one else for me, Harper. I'll beg, borrow, or kill to give you everything you ever want or need."

She was pretty sure the saying was beg, borrow, or *steal*, but hey, who was she to argue with a great speech like that? "So, that's great and all, but you haven't really asked me anything yet. Are you asking me a question?" she prompted primly, batting her eyes at him expectantly.

His smile grew. "Yes, smartass, I am." He took a deep breath. "Harper Hall, will you marry—"

"Yes!" she squealed, then threw herself into his arms.

"Thank God," he said into her hair at the same time Candy said, "I think I'm gonna be sick."

Like it so far? You can download your copy today right here:
http://amzn.to/2bgun3m

ABOUT THE AUTHOR

The normal:

Isabel Jordan writes because it's the only profession that allows her to express her natural sarcasm and not be fired. She is a paranormal and contemporary romance author. Isabel lives in the U.S. with her husband, ten-year-old son, a senile beagle, a neurotic shepherd mix, and a ginormous Great Dane mix.

The weird:

Now that the normal stuff is out of the way, here's some weird-but-true facts that would never come up in polite conversation. Isabel Jordan:

1. Is terrified of butterflies (don't judge...it's a real phobia called lepidopterophobia)
2. Is a lover of all things ironic (hence the butterfly on the cover of *Semi-Charmed*)
3. Is obsessed with *Supernatural, Game of Thrones, The Walking Dead,* and *Dog Whisperer.*
4. Hates coffee. Drinks a Diet Mountain Dew every morning.
5. Will argue to the death that *Pretty in Pink* ended all wrong. (Seriously, she ends up with the guy who was embarrassed to be seen with her and not the nice guy who loved her all along? That would

never fly in the world of romance novels.)

6. Would eat Mexican food every day if given the choice.

7. Reads two books a week in varied genres.

8. Refers to her Kindle as "the precious."

9. Thinks puppy breath is one of the best smells in the world.

10. Is a social media idgit. (Her husband had to explain to her what the point of Twitter was. She's still a little fuzzy on what Instagram and Pinterest do.)

11. Kicks ass at Six Degrees of Kevin Bacon.

12. Stole her tagline idea ("weird and proud") from her son. Her tagline idea was, "Never wrong, not quite right." She liked her son's idea better.

13. Breaks one vacuum cleaner a year because she ignores standard maintenance procedures (Really, you're supposed to empty the canister every time you vacuum? Does that seem excessive to anyone else?)

14. Is still mad at the WB network for cancelling *Angel* in 2004.

15. Can't find her way from her bed to her bathroom without her glasses, but refused eye surgery, even when someone else offered to pay. (They lost her at "eye flap". Seriously, look it up. Scary stuff.)